PRAISE FOR DEBBIE MORGAN'S WRITING

'Authentic and compelling.'
—Jimmy McGovern

'Robyn, the protagonist was great company.'
—Carol Birch

'A remarkable first novel.'
—Alan Bleasdale

'Shot through with gorgeous images and subtle humour.'
—The Guardian

'Has an emotional honesty, not easily forgotten.'
—Herald Scotland

'The strength of Morgan's writing, she has an ear for dialogue, believable characterisation and memorable imagery.'
—The Observer

'A page-turner of a story.'
—Nerve Magazine

'Touchingly well executed.'
—Library Journal

First published in 2023
by Summer Seat Press Ltd
1 Irish Square
St Asaph
LL17 ORN
United Kingdom
contact@summerseatpress.co.uk

Copyright, Deborah Morgan ©2023
The moral right of Deborah Morgan to be identified as the author of this work has been asserted by her in accordance with the Copyright, Designs and Patents Act, 1988

All rights reserved. No part of this publication may be reproduced or transmitted, in any form by any means, electronic or mechanical, including photocopying, recording or any information storage or retrieval system, without permission in writing from the publisher or a license, permitting restricted copying. In the United Kingdom such licenses are issued by the Copyright Licensing Agency, 90 Tottenham Court Road, London WIP OLP

All the characters in this book are fictitious and any resemblance to actual persons, living or dead, is purely coincidental. A CIP catalogue reference for this book is available from the British Library

Printed and bound by CPI Group
(UK) Ltd, Croydon, CR0 4YY

*This book is dedicated to my family,
their love and support is what keeps me going.
And for Bob, who will be forever missed.*

IMAGINE LIVING

Deborah Morgan x

DEBORAH MORGAN
Author of critically acclaimed novel, Disappearing Home

Summer Seat Press
EST. 2023

1

1980

If words could eat other words, then hope would be the word to eat despair. HOPE. A word that for years had protected me from myself: from thinking too much about everything lost, and everything I could still lose. The word slid across my lips, its sound full of light. I breathed in its warmth, soft as feathers under a pigeon sky.

For the first few minutes of the bus journey, I closed my eyes, the sounds of the city leaking in through narrow windows speckled with grime; the petrolly smell giving me a headache this early in the morning, grey pavements barely visible through the heavy northern mist. The bus driver, sharing his unfunny jokes with almost every person who got on, annoyed the hell out of me. I listened to his clumsy laughter flooding through the damp air; hoping Maud, my manageress, would be in a good mood today, because I was going to be late for the second time this week, in my first job.

Before she slid the pasties into the oven, Maud cupped each one in her palm like holy bread, with her other palm, dusted the muck off the top. 'You did that the other day with the sausage rolls,' she said. 'Dropped all over the floor, you need to keep your mind on the job, Robyn.'

There were days when I felt so vulnerable, like everything I said or did was wrong. This could be just one day, after months of doing my absolute best. Nan always said not to dwell on this, as it was only one fragment of who we truly are. 'Remember all the good you've done, it'll keep your feet to the ground.'

Maud slid the glass oven door shut; adjusted the dial to HOT, walked into the back of the shop to wash her hands. I'd left school, was on a six month government scheme in Waterford's bakery, where I was learning how not to drop food all over the floor. A couple of days before my interview, Nan took me for new clothes, and a blow-dry in Curl Up-n-Dye. The interview lasted three minutes. I had to show Mr Fairbrother, a man without any chin, my finger nails.

Nan was delighted I was working opposite the Adelphi Hotel. 'Our twenty-fifth wedding anniversary, we saved up, had a meal, with champagne, a room and everything, grand it was, the best night out of our lives.'

I took my breaks with Dot, so Maud could have Stella all to herself.

'You all right, Robyn?' Dot said.

I told her about Nan, and her operation coming up soon.

'You're entitled to two weeks off,' she said. 'She'll need somebody there to look after her. Go and tell Maud you need time off.'

'I've only been here two weeks.'

'So? It's not your fault she's sick.'

'I'll speak to her on my dinner break.'

'Want me to ask?' Dot said.

'No, I'll sort it later.'

'We'll be rushed off our feet later. Go and ask her now.'

Dot was finishing a cheese roll when I got back; spoke from the side of a golf ball mouth.

'Well?'

'I haven't worked enough hours to be entitled to time off. She'll ask Mr Fairbrother, but the answer will be no.'

'Really,' Dot said, smirking, 'that's how much she knows.'

The lad from Man's Gear, next door, was in the queue, looking smart in his white shirt and skinny black tie. Last week, a little kid was five pence short for a sausage roll, he dug into his pockets and handed it over. I liked that about him, it made me think he might be all right.

Dot caught my eye, smiled, gave me a wink. She'd been working it so I got to serve him. My hands shook when I passed over his change. That day, Dot served him.

While we ate our dinner, she told me his name was Alex. He went to Gatsby's every Saturday night and he hadn't got a girl.

'You found all that out?'

She nodded, scraped a line of salad cream off her chin spread it across her tongue. 'Fed up watching you dither about. By the time you make a move he'll be queuing for his pension.'

'Where's Gatsby's?'

'It'll be in town somewhere. No harm done if you and a mate go along. Have a little dance.'

'I suppose.'

'You have got a mate?'

'Rose would come.'

'You'll need a great outfit. Find out what Rose plans on wearing first.'

'Why?'

'To stand out, where lads are involved, friends or no friends, you have to destroy the competition.'

I thought about the clothes I had in Nan's. They were all a show; Dot stared at the wall, voice all far away and dreamy. 'I bought my clothes in Southport when I was your age. Delphina's the shop was called. It's not there anymore. There's bound to be another shop like Delphina's in Southport. Then nobody would have the same dress as you. You could get the train there.'

'Not on my wage.'

'The train's not dear. You might be able to pay off a frock weekly. I'll have a root later, see what I've got.'

I stared at Dot's huge chest, buttonholes busting against the strain, folded my arms across my flat chest. 'Thanks, Dot, but I'll find something.'

'Don't think my stuff would fit you anyway, you're only about a size eight.'

'I'm a ten.'

'It's all about what you're wearing and how you walk. I've seen pig-ugly women cop off with gorgeous fellas and it's all down to the clothes.' She looked at my face. 'Not that I'm saying you're ugly or anything.'

I stared into her dark eyes.

'Listen to me for God's sake,' she said. 'I'm no Marilyn Monroe.'

'Who's she?'

'Only the most beautiful blonde that ever walked the earth.'

'Like Debbie Harry?'

'Who's she?'

'The singer, Blondie.'

'Never heard of her; you want real glam, check out Marilyn Monroe. And don't forget the walk. Watch me.'

Dot had cut about six inches off the hem of her overall, so it rested just below her knickers. She straightened herself up, done a hip-swing swagger down the narrow passageway, where she met Mr Fairbrother, towards the toilet and back again.

We heard Maud calling, Dot checked her lippy in the mirror, pushed up her bra. 'Sorry love, I'll show you the walk again, next time.' She pinched my cheek. 'Oh, and makeup. I'll show you both; but don't show Rose. The sooner you get yourself courting the better. Don't have to pay for nights out once you've got a fella.'

Nan kept telling me I had to protect myself against fellas. She warned me not to have connections with any man. 'And don't go near men with moustaches,' she said, 'cos they've got something to hide.'

Nan didn't like Rose. 'She'll take you round the corner and lose you, that one.'

'But Rose's all right,' I told her. 'Never done me any harm.'

'Mark my words,' Nan said, 'she's a loose cannon.'

Early next morning Nan was in the kitchen. She'd been up half the night with the pain in her hip. 'It's half seven. What time are you in work?'

'Eight.' She looked a bit better. I got washed and dressed, shouted a quick bye and legged it for the bus.

In work, Maud tapped a fingernail on the face of her watch, the click-click of it let me know I was two minutes late. She was in a mood. Dot said it was because Maud hadn't had sex in ages, and she was that old now, her fanny grew mushrooms.

Some of the things Dot came out with made me feel sick.

After the dinner time rush, we listened to Maud tell Stella,

(Maud loved Stella but Dot thought Stella was an arse-licker), that she'd found out Mr Fairbrother was fifty at the weekend, and he threw a big party at his house. Maud and her husband, Harold, weren't invited. 'Thirty years I've worked here,' Maud said. 'They don't give two hoots. I feel like walking right out that door, leaving them in the lurch. Honestly, it's one of the worst things that ever happened to me.'

Some people lived in a world where nothing bad happened. The best thing about living in a world where bad things happened was, when something good happened, you noticed it.

Maud had headaches. Sometimes she sat in the tiny toilet at the back of the shop with a black mask over her eyes. She pulled the mask out of her overall pocket. 'I can't take this lack of appreciation any more, if I did leave here, I bet I wouldn't be missed. Part of the furniture, that's all I am.'

Stella weighed in. 'Maud, where would we find another manageress as good as you?' This made Maud smile, she touched Stella's arm, folded the mask away.

Dot shook her head, picked up a cream doughnut; stuck her tongue deep inside the split and licked; a mixture of white cream and red jam splodged on top of her thick lips. Maud caught her. 'Eat that in the back on your break. Make sure you write it down.'

We got a ten minute break in the morning and ten in the afternoon. Before she nipped to the toilet, Dot devoured her doughnut in two bites. In the small square mirror above the sink, thickened candy pink lippy back on.

'She's after Maud's job when she retires, thinks I don't know.' Dot took out a bottle of Charlie. Twisted off the top with her teeth, pinched her hem up another inch, knees bent; legs spread wide. 'Thinks Maud's gonna put a good word in with the managers, ha!' She squirted the perfume between her legs; the tiny hem slipped back down. 'What Stella doesn't know,' she said, spraying her wrists and neck, 'is that the area managers all hate Maud's guts.'

Some afternoons, when Maud went out on her forty-five minute dinner break, Mr Fairbrother parked his black Mercedes outside the shop, and, without looking at any of us, he marched straight into the back then slammed the door. After a couple of minutes he'd shout, 'Dot, can you come out here, I need to see the books.' Dot patted her hair in place, done a hip-swing swagger past Stella, winked at me.

'Slag,' Stella said under her breath; then slower, 'dirty-fat-slag.'

I'd seen Dot come out of the back with her face flushed red, and a long ladder up the front of her tights. Stella would barge past her. 'It's not my fault,' Dot would shout after her, 'men find me utterly irresistible.'

A couple of days later, Dot had a right mood on when she came back from being with Mr Fairbrother. She caught Stella shaking her head. 'Don't know why you're looking so shocked, bet you've done it up a back alley, cheeks of your arse rubbed raw against the brick wall.'

Stella moved in close to Dot. 'You can shag in the passageway all you want, eat half the stock while Maud's on her breaks, but don't start being a bitch, or I'll ram your head inside that oven; turn the dial to hot, slam the doors against your thick fucking throat.'

Then Stella walked away from Dot calling back, 'Don't worry, my day will come.' As if that wasn't bad enough, they'd rough-eye each other all week, in dry ragged blasts, and when they'd go out, the slam of the shop door made the glass window shiver inside its frame.

When women got that angry, and that awful rage came, it was deep down scary, like every terrible thing life had flung at them spilled out all at once, in the wrong place. Days like this had me wishing I worked someplace else.

2

Saturday was my day off. Sometimes I'd go and sit in Curl Up-n-Dye. Help make cups of tea for the customers, watch Rose shampoo hair and brush up. I loved the smell of shampoo and hairspray, and seeing how the women left the salon, hair all clean and shiny, feeling and looking lifted.

On her dinner, Rose pulled a yellow trolley up to a chair, wound rollers onto a plastic head with wild black hair.

'Coming to the disco on Friday night?' I asked.

'It's full of little kids.'

'I know, but we haven't been for ages and it's something to do.'

'It's boring, now.'

'Ah, come on, just this once, we'll have a laugh.'

Friday, I paid my fifty pence to get in, looked around for Rose. It was dark inside, Blondie's *Heart of Glass* played. I felt like getting up to dance but it was a stupid idea. Everyone was about ten. This was a place I used to feel small in.

I wondered what had happened to her. Checked the toilets

but there was no sign. Outside, on my way back to the bus stop, there she was, down a side street all dressed up, white blouse, high heels, faded denim mini skirt. There was a boy with her. They were kissing. He had his hand up the front of her skirt.

'Rose, you okay?'

She pulled away from him, staggered towards me. As she got nearer I could see her eyes all far away and wobbly.

'What've you had?'

'Nothing.'

'She's with me,' the lad said, sticking out his pigeon chest. Rose rummaged about in her bag; pulled out an empty half bottle of vodka, waved it in the air. 'Look what Simmo gave me.'

Simmo grinned, looked down at the floor. He wore a dark blue Fred Perry shirt and Levi jeans, on his feet dark blue Kickers to match his top. He had a thin light brown moustache, that looked like it would blow away if the wind picked up.

'Have you had all that?'

'No. Only what was in the bottle.' She giggled. 'I spilled some. Simmo had the brandy.'

I took her arm. 'C'mon let's go for a walk.'

Simmo followed us. I made my voice hard, 'On our own.'

Rose's heel got caught in a cracked bit of pavement. Simmo tried to help. 'Beat it,' I said.

We walked away, she waved at him. 'See you Simmo, lad.'

Sitting on the bench inside the bus stop next to Rose, Simmo was behind us propped up against a shop window. I couldn't let her go home like this, her mum and dad would go mad. We could sit on the bus until the last stop. Get another bus back again.

When it came Simmo tried to get on. I told the driver that we didn't know him, and he was following us. The driver edged out of his seat, leaned over his little silver door and pointed a thick finger at Simmo. 'Friggin' pervert,' he said. 'Sling your hook.' He smiled at me. 'Pervy little swine; got two daughters myself at home.'

Simmo walked back towards the disco.

We sat down. 'Jesus, Rose, what're you playing at?'

She rested her head on my shoulder. 'He's all right, lives in our street.'

'He had his hand up your skirt.'

'Did he?'

'You know he did. That's horrible.'

'Don't tell anyone.'

'I won't.'

'Promise?'

'I promise.'

A couple of hours later, we turned into Snowfield Street. Simmo was waiting. Rose was a bit better by then; she walked up to him and slapped his face hard. 'You keep your dirty hands to yourself.'

He covered the slap with the palm of his hand, didn't look at me when he spoke. 'You weren't complaining till she turned up.' He legged it down the street.

The following Friday Rose waited for me outside the disco. She had a small bottle of vodka in her bag and a tube of wild cherry lippy. 'Wanna go the park?' she said, holding out the lippy to me.

'I thought you wanted to go back the disco?'

'Have you seen it in there? They're all little kids, only short of Andy frigging Pandy.'

'We could just listen to the music and watch.'

'That's boring. Let's go the shop, buy a can of coke and drink this.'

We sat on a bench in the park, swigged down vodka and coke in two little paper cups. Simmo and another lad were walking around the park, they disappeared inside trees.

'You knew he was gonna be here?'

'No.'

'Liar.'

'So?'

She poured herself another vodka and coke, tonnes more vodka than coke. I put a hand over the top of my cup.

Rose grabbed my hand. 'I know, let's follow them.'

'What's the matter with you?'

'Nothing's the matter with me, it's you.'

Rose lifted the cup to her lips took a big gulp, pulled a face. 'God, that's strong. You don't even know him, give him a chance,' she said.

'Neither do you and you let him shove his arm up your top.'

'No I never,' she took another swig. 'I let him shove his hand up my skirt.'

'I'm not picking you up when you're too pissed to walk, or taking you on bus rides until you sober up.'

She carried on drinking. Took the wild cherry lippy from her bag, got more on her face than her lips.

'Bore!' Rose's voice was rough; her breath hot on my face; stinking like dry sand. 'I said you're boring.'

They walked past us, arm-in-arm doing a funny legs-straight-out-in-front-walk. Rose giggled.

Simmo's mate said, 'Evening ladies.'

'Did you see the way Simmo's mate looked at you?'

'Boring? Because I won't drink vodka and let some pervy lad shove his arm up my skirt?'

'I reckon he fancies you.'

'Who?'

'Simmo's mate; just look at him, properly, he's gorgeous and if you don't fancy him, if you really, really really don't, we'll go.'

Rose's eyes were all wobbly, again.

I stood. 'I'm going to Nan's. Coming?'

'But Simmo's brought a mate.'

'I'm going, now.' I grabbed hold of her arm. 'Come on.'

She shook her head, pushed me away. 'I'm staying.'

'Rose?'

'I said I'm staying. You can't tell me what to do.'

I took her by the arm again. 'Come on.'

She pulled away. 'I've said no. Now piss off, you bore.'

'Fine, do what you want.'

'I frigging-well will.'

It was dark when I got to Nan's and my head was spinning from the vodka. I felt happy though, my whole body was relaxed. I let myself in, got the pillow and blankets and fell fast asleep on the settee.

Next morning, Nan's shouting woke me up. 'You left the front door open last night, anything could've happened.'

My back was killing me and the back of my neck where I'd slept funny.

'Any lunatic could have got in. Don't know where your mind is half the time. I'm going the shop. You heard from your mother?'

'No.'

Mum lived in Edinburgh now with this fella. She hadn't heard from the man who had battered us for years. Someone told her he'd been ran over and killed, which made her smile. I'd been living with Nan since I was fourteen. Owen, the fella Mum lived with in Edinburgh, had his own pub. They met in the Grafton while he was on his mate's birthday night out.

A few months later, she moved in with him. They lived upstairs in the foot hospital. I didn't know what the pub's real name was, but that was what Mum called it, as nearly everybody in there had gout.

She asked me to move in, start at a new school and everything, but I said no, didn't want to leave my friend, Rose. I loved it at Nan's, even though she only had one bedroom and I had to sleep on the settee, she was funny and kind, and I never wanted to leave. And anyway, Mum hardly listened to a word I said.

May was the only person who encouraged me to find my father, she told me everybody was allowed one mistake in life, and most people deserved a second chance.

It was just like Nan to say that, to never give up on a person, no matter what. 'It's the hard things in life change us, Robyn, often for the better.' It was her way of thinking about my dad that made me determined one day to find him, no matter how harsh that meeting might be.

3

It was lunch time when I got to Curl Up-n-Dye. Women sat in chairs along two walls, some with royal blue towels across their shoulders. Paula, the boss, switched off the hairdryer, spoke to me through her mirror.

'Where's tilly mint?'

I shrugged.

'Cheeky mare hasn't turned in. I'm rushed off my feet, hasn't sent word or nothing. She'd better not start this lark. That's why I got rid of her Rita, pulling sickies all the time.' She turned her drier back on, shouted above the noise. 'When you see her, pass on this message, unless the house went on fire, or she was trampled on by some hairy-arsed elephant, tell Rose from me, she's sacked. On second thoughts, grab that brush and give the floor a once over before you go.'

Half past four it was by the time I got out. I legged it to Snowfield Street. Rose's mum answered the door; you could see blue and purple veins in her legs. 'Been in bed all day, still there now, says she's sick. Not feeling too good myself. Do us a favour and let Paula know. Don't want our Rose to lose her job; and she can't stand our Rita, doesn't take much to upset that moaning cow.'

By the time I got back to the shop, Paula was outside locking the door. I told her Rose was sick.

'Not nice though is it, Mrs Flanagan's been in for a set, she lives right next door, wouldn't have taken much to get word to me. I'd have been snookered without you.' Paula took a five pound note out her purse, five pounds, though, held it out to me. I couldn't believe it.

'Are you sure?' I didn't take it.

'You earned it, I owe you one.'

'Rose isn't really sacked is she?'

'Here,' she pushed the folded fiver in my palm. 'Come back next Saturday, just in case. Be here at nine, can't rely on anyone in business.' She dropped the keys inside her bag.

'What about Rose?'

'Have to see how I feel,' she said, crossing the road, coat flapping behind her. 'I'm not running a frigging charity.'

On the way home I nipped in the club opposite Nan's. She went there sometimes for an hour, met up with people she knew. Inside, there was a man cleaning behind the bar, and a fruit machine flashing its Christmas colours in the corner; on the other side of the room, a woman in a yellow overall lifted boxes of crisps out of the small cupboard.

I loved having my own money. Nan had always worked. She told me never to rely on a man for money, no matter what; a woman had to earn her own living, stand on her own two feet.

'We're not open yet,' he said. His thick, red moustache had a white line of froth across it.

'Can I buy two bottles of Guinness for my nan?'

'Who's your nan?'

'May, she lives opposite.'

'You'll get me shot,' he said, smoothed out a Kwik Save bag with his palm and stood the bottles inside.

'She's a character, May. They all love her in here, heart of gold she has, brings sandwiches and sausage rolls in every Saturday night, too kind for her own good.' The bottles clanged as he pushed them inside the bag. 'Not the same without Dan though, is she? The corner under the telly looks odd without them.'

Dan was Nan's friend. He got sick, couldn't remember stuff like people's names. His daughter, Karen, put him in a nursing home but he died a few months later. Nan missed him loads.

On her last birthday, she had too many bottles of Guinness in the club. Brought this fella home, who'd told her he had nobody to wash his shirts. I was asleep, took me ages to get comfy. I had a right nark on when they woke me up. He took his coat off and flung it towards a chair, but missed, it landed on the floor. Sid his name was, or Ted, can't remember. 'I've asked May to marry me,' he said all gooey-eyed and swaying.

'Have you now?' I said, picking his coat up and throwing it at him. 'You'll have to ask her husband first. He'll be home in a minute.' He went the colour of mashed potato and left.

I had murder with Nan the next morning. Giving me loads about connections and not going near fellas, then she brings one home. I said she couldn't go that club any more if that's the way she was going to carry on. This made her howl, she laughed so much; tears ran down her cheeks. In the end I couldn't help but join in. Nan said I had to stop as she wanted a pee. 'He-had-nobody-to-wash-his-shirts,' I laughed. This set Nan off laughing even louder.

'I wonder what the excuse will be next week; maybe he'll want you to take a drag on his ciggy? Or pee in his toilet?' I'd never seen her laugh that much. She nearly choked.

After work, I got to Nan's; there was a note on the floor. It said: Robyn, knock at Betty's. Betty answered the door with pink rollers in her hair covered over with a pink net. I could smell hairspray. She shouted back down the hall. 'Turn that telly low, Larry.'

'Sorry, love, the doctor's sent May to hospital. Months she's been waiting for her operation, the pain's unbearable now.'

'What hospital?'

'Fazakerley, nothing to worry about, Robyn, love, she'll be okay.'

A sour, acidy taste formed in my mouth. 'Can you walk in any time?'

'No, visiting time's about half six, I think. She said for you to go up and see her tomorrow, she'll be sleeping.'

Inside the walls were white, the nurse's uniforms were white, the same white square tiles everywhere. It was like going to visit somebody in heaven. It reeked at the same time sweet and sharp, disinfectant and sprouts. The air dried up your mouth.

I took the stairs to the second floor to Nan's ward, 2C. She was asleep. There were other people on the ward. One woman moaning in her sleep; her moans got louder until a nurse came and pulled the green curtain around her bed. The beds were too close together. After a little while, Nan opened her eyes. She smiled when she saw me, sat up.

'You okay, Nan?'

'I'm fine, love, going down for the operation tomorrow. Don't trust these bloody doctors.' She touched my sleeve. 'You're soaked. Get yourself an umbrella.'

I wished Nan could walk out of there, come back home with me. 'Can't they just give you a pill or something?'

'Not for this, love.'

'What time are you going down?'

'Early morning, nine, I think the nurse said. I feel tired, can't have anything to eat.' Nan didn't stop yawning. 'It'll all be worth it though, if it means this pain leaves me.'

'Can I bring you anything?'

'Just yourself, if you need money-'

'I've got money.'

'That'll be pennies. There's food in the cupboard plenty of tinned stuff, ham and corned beef. Buy yourself a small sliced on the way home. There's a jar-'

'I'll be okay. You worry about yourself. Shall I tell Mum?' I had a piece of paper with the phone number to the foot hospital written on it.

'No need. I won't be here that long.'

I hated leaving her, could tell she was worried, trying to hide it from me, chatting away, telling me what everybody was in there for. I didn't listen; was too busy thinking of ways to make her room more comfy for when she got home. A new pillow, I thought, I'll pop into TJ's, get her a new pillow.

Next day after work, I went back to the hospital. Nan was sitting up in bed.

'They had to cancel, something about a shortage of staff. It could be another week now.'

'That's awful.'

'At least I can eat again. Don't want you coming up here every night in bad weather, after being on your feet all day. Bus fares and everything to fork out, I worry about you getting home.' She smoothed down the creases on her hospital gown. 'Come back in a few days, it should all be over with by then. And double check you've locked the front door at night.'

Nan looked older; the lines on her face deeper. I said nothing, didn't want to upset her before the operation. I wasn't sleeping well.

'Robyn, come on now, straighten that face, I'll be okay.'

'I know you're strong, Nan, but you're all I've got.'

'And I'm not going anywhere. You've always got yourself to rely on. Give us a smile before you go?'

'I bought you a new pillow from TJ's on my dinner; it's lovely and soft.'

Nan reached across and hugged me and it felt good.

'Don't think too much about bad things, eh, imagine living your best life, now what would that look like?'

'I don't know; a life without too many mistakes, where I can make good choices?'

'That's my girl; always think things through a bit.'

'Can we go down the Pier Head once you're better, feed the birds; ride on the ferry?'

'And a nice cuppa in the café?'

'Yeah, I'd like that.'

'From what I've seen with people in the club, it's not a fast recovery with the hip.' She stuck out her elbow. 'When I'm climbing on the bus, you'll need to hold my feathers, girl.'

I stuck my elbow out. 'All right, only if you hold mine,' and we both laughed.

When I got home, Betty had left a note under for me to give her a knock. She opened her front door holding a plate with another plate on top. 'I thought it was you. Here, a nice shepherd's pie with gravy and veg. Can't have you wasting away, there's not enough of you as it is.'

'Thanks,' I said, taking the warm plate, knowing I couldn't stomach food right now.

'How is she?'

'All right, they had to cancel the operation.'

'Doesn't surprise me, with all the cuts Thatcher's making. It's the likes of us that'll suffer. She's gonna slice this country in half, you watch. If you need anything you know where I am. You told your mother?'

I felt the bottom of the plate burning my hand, the cloth must have slipped. 'No, Nan said not to. She doesn't want any fuss.'

Downstairs, my body slumped hard against the wall. Oh my God. If anything happened to her, though? I couldn't live with Mum, controlling my every move like she always had, but nothing would happen, she'd get well, May, she was strong, would live to be eighty or something at least. She must.

In many ways I felt guilty for being selfish, thought about how Nan leaving this world would slice me in half, just as much as being left here on my own would.

4

Next morning on our break, Dot had the makeup bag out but I wasn't taking any notice.

'If that Ron Fairbrother thinks I'm gonna settle for romance in a nasty narrow passageway, he's got another thing coming, and I've told him straight. From the way things are going with us, he'll ask me to marry him soon. I'll be able to move on from that misery I'm with now.'

In the mirror, she dusted white powder all over her face. 'Maybe the Adelphi; I've always wanted a room at the Adelphi, it all takes so long up a passageway when layers are involved, and the reek of pine bleach from the bog swimming up your nostrils. Honest to God, kills the passion, Robyn.'

She took out her bag of tricks. I couldn't get the hang of it, putting makeup on. Dot said if I wanted a fella, it was an important skill to learn. 'Who says I want a fella?' I said.

Dot laughed. 'Don't come that with me. I've seen you drooling over him. Get in front of that, now.'

She shuffled me up close to the mirror.

'Right, now pay attention, you're miles away today.' She

shook the foundation bottle, squirted a teardrop onto the back of her hand.

'Just a touch's enough, to even out the skin.'

With the pad of her finger she circled the tiny pool until it was flat. 'Now, tap it, nose first then outward, little by little, like this.' She showed me using one side of my face. Finished, she checked her watch. 'You try on the other side.'

I did exactly the same as Dot but it was all patchy. 'You'll get better; don't want it to look caked.' She gave me an old half-empty bottle of makeup out of her bag. 'Have a go at home, and understand, lipstick is a weapon no woman should be without!'

She glossed up her lips again. 'By the way, Ron said you can have the week off; let Maud know the date for the op.'

'Ron?'

'Mr Fairbrother.'

'Did he say that?'

'I just said he did, didn't I?' She nudged me out of the way with her hip; I turned fast and hugged her tight, already thinking of shopping for lamb chops and cooking roast potatoes, Nan's favourites. 'I owe you one.'

Back at the counter, Maud said her and Stella were nipping out for a minute. Dot turned the oven down, rearranged the meat pies. As soon as they left, Dot bent the silver foil away from a custard tart, eased it up to her lips. 'Mmmm,' she said, 'take something, sod writing down everything we eat. We should get our dinner for free.'

I thought she was right, but it wasn't up to Maud, she was only the manageress. Dot clicked her fingers at me. 'Hurry up, dolly daydreamer. The lovers'll be back in a minute.'

'I don't want anything,' I said.

'Then I'll have something for you.' She shoved another custard tart into her mouth. When she'd finished, bits of pastry and blobs of custard sat on her face. I smiled.

'What?' she said.

'Nothing.'

'What?'

'Go and look in the mirror.'

Just as Dot left, Alex walked in. Even before he spoke I could feel my face burn. 'Yes, please?' I said.

'Can of coke and a cheese pasty, please.'

I slipped the pasty into a paper bag took a can of coke from the fridge.

Dot had cleaned her face, 'Hello, lad, Robyn was saying, Alex, she's going to Gatsby's on Saturday with her mate.'

He looked at me, 'Yeah?'

I said nothing.

'Isn't it up by the courts?'

'It's on Victoria Street.'

'You there on Saturday?'

'Yeah, I'm going with my mate, Harry.'

'They've never been before, Robyn and…'

'Rose,' I said.

'Could you show them what's what?'

Alex looked confused. 'What's what?'

'You know the toilets and the bar and…'

'She's messing,' I said, 'stop messing about, Dot.'

'Oh, okay,' he said, and left the shop.

'What did you say that for? Made me sound like a child; show me where the toilets are.'

Dot laughed. 'They have to be led by the bloody nose to do anything, lads. You can tell the ones who've had their mothers still wiping their arses at fifteen. Get yourself to Southport on Saturday and see what's what over a classy dress.'

Alex didn't come back in for the rest of the week. One dinner time, I spotted him passing the shop window eating a burger from the Wimpy. I thought Dot had messed up my chance, if there ever was a chance. I wondered what Nan might say when I told her about him, she probably wouldn't be happy.

Betty brought me my tea every night, reminded me to lock the front door.

'She'll be out soon.'

'I can't wait,' I said.

At night, in the place alone, I'd listen to the peaceful hour on the radio, which began at midnight. People putting requests on for someone they fancied, love songs: *Cruising on a Sunday Afternoon*. I dreamed of the day someone might put one on for me. That would probably never happen, but it didn't stop me dreaming.

Saturday morning, I was on the Southport train. I'd left five pounds keep for Nan at home.

Inside the big department stores, the word that came into my mind when I looked at the price tags was, *unfriendly*. This was the second shop I'd been in, and there was no way I could afford to buy anything that looked half-decent.

It was different here to our city centre, people seemed to walk slower, and the pavements were spotless. Reaching Lord Street, I wandered into a second-hand shop. On the farthest dress rail, I found a gorgeous pink and green paisley print dress, with box pleats at the bottom. Inside the label said, *Jaeger*.

'Can I help you?' the lady said. She stooped, arranged earrings and brooches inside a glass cabinet. Her hands were thin and veiny, like Nan's, but she didn't look very old in her face.

'Is it okay if I try this?'

She straightened up; had lovely grey, blue eyes that slanted upwards. Her silver-blonde hair was twisted into a soft bun at the nape of her neck. 'Yes, the changing room is through here.'

She pulled a brown curtain back and walked away, 'Let me see it on you,' she called back. 'You've got an eye for a bargain. That's silk.'

I smiled at myself in the mirror, the colours were perfect.

'How is it?'

I pulled back the brown curtain. She tugged at the dress. 'It's a bit big around the waist. Give me a minute.'

She came back with a thin pink waspie belt, fastened it around my waist. 'All you need to do is baggy the dress over the belt a bit. You really suit the colours.'

It looked like a different dress. 'The belt makes it look much better,' I said. 'Thank you.'

When I lifted it over my head there was a musty smell on the lining. 'Can I wash it?' I shouted through the curtain.

'Yes. You can hand wash silk in lukewarm water. Let it dripdry on the line. Soak it in fabric conditioner in the bath, or a mild baby shampoo, to make it smell nice. Once it's dry, you can put the box-pleats back in easily with the iron and brown paper. Make sure it's a warm iron, not hot.'

Back outside I handed her the dress, 'Brown paper?'

'It stops any damage to the fabric, keeps away that greasy shine. Don't move the iron backwards and forwards. Just set the pleat in place, cover it with brown paper and drop the iron onto it, press, and then lift the iron off. It will look as good as new.'

There were three second-hand shops on Lord Street. I searched in all three, but the first shop, where the lady was helpful was the best, so I headed back there for one last root. Inside, I had a look at the handbags. A black one took my eye; shaped like a circle, two loopy thick handles. I unfastened the gold clasp, looked inside. There was one of those compact things, on the lid pink roses and exotic birds, all outlined in royal blue. I pushed in the button and a mirror opened up. The lady walked towards me. 'Back again?'

'I found this inside the bag.' She took hold of it.

'It's an old Stratton compact, probably from the nineteen-fifties,' she clicked it closed. 'It's lost much of its gilding, the base looks rather sorry for itself.' It had worn away, the gold, and bits of green had started to replace it. 'Where's the powder?'

Another circle flipped up once the lid was fully open. She lifted that and I could see a flat spongy pad, she moved it out of the way, tan-coloured pressed powder sat around the edges, the middle bit had been dabbed clean, you could see the silver bottom. 'See how the second cover released itself? That inner clasp pulls back automatically, to stop the lady chipping her nail polish. Exquisite, don't you think?'

'I love it. Will I need to pay any extra?'

'No, the bag's bought as seen.'

'I'm glad I came back in,' I said.

'Wash the bag down with soapy water and a damp sponge, especially the handles. It'll work lovely with the dress and black shoes; new shoes. Never buy second-hand shoes.'

'I've got a pair of black shoes.'

'Good. You're all set then.'

I thanked the lady for her help and headed to the station.

Rose was brushing up when I got there, flipped her eyes for me to follow her into the back. Paula was blow-drying the last customer. She smiled through the mirror.

'All right, Robyn.'

'Hiya,'

'Sorry,' Rose said.

'What for?'

'Acting like a divvy.'

'It's all right. Was everything okay?'

'Yeah, I left not long after you.'

'I knocked the next day, but you were sick.'

'Paula's kicked off on me, says I'm sacked if I leave her in the lurch again, she said it was you saved my job, got me another chance, thanks.' She hugged me.

I smiled through the mirror at Paula; she smiled back.

'Fancy coming out tonight?'

'Where?'

'To a club?'

'What club?'

'Gatsby's, in town, don't wanna drink, to dance?'

'Town though, everyone gets dressed up. I've seen our Rita before she goes to Cindy's. I've got nothing to wear.'

'Borrow something off your Rita.'

'She won't let me.'

'What time does she go out?'

'About ten.'

'We'll go out later. Lend something out of her wardrobe and put it back when you get home.'

'Not sure about a nightclub, though, and getting home afterwards, we mightn't get in.'

'Everyone our age is going now. We can walk home from town, what is it, twenty minutes?'

It was like a hollow part of my life needed filling out. I wanted to try doing something different with the weekends, had this fear that if I stood still for too long everyone who was important in my life would move on and leave me behind, like my real dad did.

'Or you could come to mine, Rose. I'm nearer to town?'

'Nah, your nan hates me.'

'Nan won't be in. She's in hospital having an operation, and she doesn't hate you.'

Her face flushed, 'Sorry to hear that.'

I thought about how tired she'd looked the last time I saw her, thought again about her laughing with me, about bringing that man home from the club.

'She'll be out soon, stronger than ever. Will you come?'

'All right, see you at half ten.'

5

I bought myself curry, rice and chips with peas, from poison Kenny's; didn't buy fish. Nan had told me too many people had done that, ended up with their backsides glued to the toilet seat all weekend. I hardly ate anything.

There was no time to wash the dress so I sprayed the lining with some of Nan's Yardley Lavender; sprayed it all over the belt, too, hung it in the bathroom.

Slipping in Nan's bed, I stretched my arms and legs right out, wriggled my body up and down the mattress. Lay flat on my back and closed my eyes, her lavender smell made me feel warm. The last thing I remembered was the sound of Nan's clock ticking away.

It was Rose shouting my name through the letterbox that woke me. She looked lovely in cream canvas trousers with legwarmers, and a white shirt. She had red beads draped from her right shoulder across to her side, red loopy earrings and red high heels to match. 'You look amazing,' I said.

'Thanks, I've raided our Rita's wardrobe, hurry up or it'll be a waste of time going.'

I got a quick bath, washed my hair and tried to get the tinted moisturiser to go on right, couldn't get it even like Dot did but tried not to cake it.

Rose shouted through the bathroom door, 'Anything in to drink?'

'Drop of port in the bottom cupboard.'

'Can I have some?'

'Help yourself. There's lemonade by the bread bin, might be a bit flat, though. I'll be out now.'

When I opened the kitchen door, Rose was drinking port straight from the bottle. She clunked it down on the table.

'Never had port before, it's good, fruity, wanna drop?' She turned around, took a breath, her face fell. 'Ahh, erm, oh, your dress looks...' She scrambled for the words. 'Well, different.'

'It's one of Nan's old ones,' I lied, grabbing my handbag.

There were loads of teenagers waiting for the last bus into town. Rose knew one of the girls; her mum got her hair done in Curl Up-n-Dye. She asked Rose where we were going and she told them.

The girl shook her head. 'It's dead hard getting into Gatsby's, the bouncers are horrible. You have to look eighteen. We all got the knock back last week. They'll let anyone in Cindy's. If you don't get in, make your way there.'

The bus came. We sat downstairs; they all went upstairs to smoke. Rose sat in front of me, stretched her legs out across both seats.

'What if we don't get in?'

'Do you think I look eighteen?'

She took the wild cherry lippy out of her bag. 'Here, put some of this on, it'll make you look older. And stick your chest out when we get to the main door. We have to get in. I can't go near Cindy's, our Rita will kill me. She's only wore these clothes once.'

'Stick out what chest, looks like my head's on backwards?' I said. Rose couldn't stop laughing.

The lady who took our money on the door, and the bouncers, didn't give us a second look. They were too busy with some lad who was demanding to see his girlfriend, Carla, a barmaid who had chucked him.

Inside, the place was enormous. The dance floor was up on a platform with a gigantic silver ball above it. Girls danced to Bryan Ferry: *Dance Away*, with their handbags on the floor in front of their feet. There were lads dancing too, with girls; and lads dancing together, messing about. The carpet felt spongy under my feet. On my skin; tiny fizzes, like when bits of a sparkler dripped on you at bonfire night. Rose's, mouth was wide open.

'Won't find Andy frigging Pandy in here,' she said. 'God, it's amazing, Robyn, look!'

I shouted above the music. 'What?'

'Look.'

'At what?'

'You must be able to see it.'

'See what, is your Rita here?'

'Can't believe I've been settling for lads around that divvy little disco. Look at them, Robyn.' She opened a couple of her buttons. 'Wall-to-wall fabulous lads; fabulicious, that's what this place should be called; fabu-friggin'-licious.'

Rose found a space on the dance floor. Shouted, come on, to me. The music was loud and the lights were flashing. Rita had told her all about sex two years ago, though some of it I didn't believe. She dropped her bag in front of her feet and started dancing, red beads swishing from side-to- side. I followed her onto the dance floor, laughing. She took my hands in her hands, shouted at me. 'This is fantastic, I love it here.'

I felt lighter in my bones.

Rose looked across at a gang of lads standing by the bar. One of them lifted his glass at her and winked. 'Anything could happen tonight, Robyn,' she said, undoing another one of her buttons, 'anything at all.' Two lads were dancing in front of us. I wanted to burst out laughing, was glad I couldn't see Rose's face. At the disco, they'd watch you for a couple of weeks before they got you up; made sure you weren't going to walk away.

The lad dancing with me kept looking behind, messing about with his mate. When he turned back towards me, looking right into my face, I looked away, across to the other side of the room. Afraid he'd see something he didn't like and walk off the dance floor. When the record finished, I was relieved to see Rose's smiling face.

'They got us up first dance,' she said, breathless. 'Some girls don't get a dance all night our Rita said. Did you see how many girls had to dance with girls? Not us. They were all jealous, looking over.' Her eyes went all sparkly.

'All right, Rose. It was only a dance.'

The next record came on and I saw two different lads, pointing at us. 'Come to the toilet with me?'

'Be quick. Don't wanna miss a minute.'

Inside the toilets, a line of girls stood in front of the wide mirror; stroked mascara onto lashes, yanked up bra straps, thickened lips in lippy. I came out of the cubicle. Rose cupped her hands under the tap, slurped up water. 'Hey, Robyn,' she shouted, 'I just had my first drink in Gatsby's.'

'Divvy little kids,' a red-haired girl, putting orange lippy on said to her mate.

'You talking about me?' Rose said.

'Piss off,' orange lippy said. 'Get back in your pram.'

Rose pushed her hard in the back.

I panicked. 'C'mon, Rose, let's dance.' The girl looked shocked, but tried to make a joke. 'Whoooo,' orange lippy said, her eyes crawling up and down my dress. 'C'mon now, Rose, do as you're told, or Bette Davis will kill your fuckin' budgie.'

All of her mates were laughing. 'Horrible witch,' I said, pulling Rose out of the toilets.

Rose said, 'I should've taken that orange lippy, rammed it straight down her smarmy throat.'

'Take no notice, she's not worth us getting kicked out, I really wanna dance, mess about, just me and you. Sod the fellas.'

'Cheeky cow; she's only about eighteen herself. Thinks she's a woman. She's not making a show of me. I'm gonna get her.'

Jesus. She went on and on. Probably the only thing Rose loved better than lads was a good fight. In school, she fought girls, one and two years older than herself. She was always first there once a fight broke out on the playground, ended up a kind of referee in our last year. Younger girls would come over after a fight and ask Rose who she thought had won. She would stand between the two girls, give a blow-by-blow account of what she'd seen, then end by saying to one of the girls, 'Based on what I saw, you definitely got absolutely fuckin' battered.'

The winner would walk away wearing a big smile like a badge. So when Rose said she was gonna get that girl from the toilets, I had to distract her, because I knew she meant it.

Back on the dance floor, she kept looking around, not at the lads now but at the girls. When two lads got us up to dance, this time I was made up. The lads didn't walk away once the record stopped. 'Staying up?' he asked. I tilted my head to the side saw Rose chatting to her lad, 'okay.'

'You been anywhere before here?'

'No you?'

'A few places; Scarlett's bar, the Vaults.'

I didn't have a clue where he meant, 'Any good?'

'The usual, you know, packed, everyone pissed.'

'Hate that.'

'You hate it? That's why we go out. Wanna drink?'

'I'm okay.'

'Haven't seen you two in here before?'

Because the music was so loud he leaned in close when he spoke, his breath reeked of old carpet slippers. It would've been so much easier if I could've just danced with Rose.

What if a girl was to do that? I imagined going over to a lad I liked the look of, a lad standing against the wall with his mates, and me starting to dance, dropping my bag down at his feet looking him in the eyes, and boogying, saying: *Haven't seen you in here before?* The idea made me smile.

'What's the joke?' the lad asked.

'What?'

'The joke: something funny?'

'No.'

He checked his fly. 'What's funny? You're laughing at me, aren't you?'

'No, I'm not.'

He stopped dancing. 'Skinny slag,' he said and walked off the dance floor.

Rose saw him walk away; stopped dancing, said something to his mate.

35

'What's the matter?'

'Don't know. He-'

'Come on, he's just made a holy show of us, that divvy, let's go the bar.'

We stood there for ages before being served. Rose ordered two glasses of cider and black. 'That's what our Rita and her mates drink, it lasts longer than a short,' she said.

It tasted okay. 'You know what, Rose, every time you say we're gonna have a laugh we don't. Stop saying that.'

The night rushed away from us, they were playing the last record when I saw him. People had already copped off and left Gatsby's.

'Hiya, Alex,' I said. He looked up and smiled. 'All right er…'

'Robyn,' I said. 'From Waterford's, this is Rose.'

He nodded at the lad sitting next to him.

'Harry,' he said.

Rose's mouth fell open when she spied Harry; her words were hot in my ear. 'Frrriiiigggg! What did you say about leaving the lads for tonight? You've got no chance, now, he's gorgeous.'

The bar closed and the bouncers came over and ordered us out. We took a walk through town and ended up in Chinatown.

'Wanna go for something to eat?' Alex said.

Harry said, 'I'm skint.'

I gave what money I had left, so did Rose. Alex didn't need taxi money because he lived near town. He counted it all out, said we had enough money to order one meal between two.

We ordered curried chicken with egg fried rice and a portion of chips. The lads ordered a beef curry. For our drinks we had tap water. I sat opposite Alex, Rose sat opposite Harry. By accident my knee brushed against Alex's, and he smiled.

'You two get any girls up to dance?' Rose asked.

'Nah, couldn't be bothered, I've got two left feet,' Alex said.

'Thought I didn't see you two on the dance floor.'

'You wouldn't anyway, it was packed.'

'Still would've spotted you two a mile off, wouldn't we, Robyn?'

I said nothing.

When we'd finished eating, the waiter brought these thin white tube things with steam rising off them. Rose picked one up with her knife and fork, and tried to slice it open. Alex and Harry stared at her. She sawed away at that thing with her knife; stabbed it with her fork, steam clouded her face, made her fringe go all floppy.

'Rubbery friggers these pancakes,' she said, 'don't think they're cooked right.'

Rose looked up, watched the lads unfold the hot flannels and wipe their hands. Her mouth made the shape of an O and she swore. Alex and Harry cracked up laughing.

It had gone four in the morning by the time me we got back to Nan's. I ran into the bathroom first for a pee. Rose shouted for me to turn the light off.

'Wanna little snack?' I asked, carrying a rolled up white bath towel under my arm.

'Frig off, you. Bet you didn't know what they were for. Felt like an absolute div.'

She was right. I didn't.

Rose slept with a blanket over her, on the two-seater settee. 'I'm full up on love, Robyn, my mate,' she shouted through the wall, 'full up on luuurrrvvvve.'

The last thing I heard was her laughing like a madwoman, and I joined in. Rose was still howling through the wall half an hour later.

6

Monday morning. 'Any luck in Southport?'

'I got a dress,' I said, too embarrassed to mention it was second-hand.

Dot whipped the skimpy overall out of her bag, 'Brilliant, and Gatsby's?'

'I went with Rose.'

'And?'

'Alex was there.'

'Get a move on you two,' Maud shouted from the front counter. 'Stella's doing everything out here.'

Dot fastened her buttons, pushed her breasts up high; stuck two fingers up through the wall at Maud.

'Oh my God, he walked you home didn't he?'

'Not exactly, we went for a meal.'

'You got a meal out of him on your first date?'

It was Dot's astonished look that made me say what I said next, to stretch it that bit further.

'And he took me to a party, his boss's birthday party, at the Adelphi Hotel.'

'You're a dark horse all right; the Adelphi, though? What's it like?'

'Chandeliers everywhere; and maroon carpets that bounce off the soles of your shoes, and a live band, saxophones and everything, candles on all the tables, men with silver trays, wearing bow ties and white shirts, with gloves to match, carrying free champagne with a strawberry perched on the side of every glass.' I took a breath; had remembered it all from an old film.

Dot's eyes were huge, 'You had champagne?'

'I did and the bubbles went up my nose.'

'Bloody hell, I've never tasted champagne, don't know what to say.'

'And the dresses; a woman sitting next to me had black satin gloves on, right up to her elbows. And when she sipped her champagne, her little finger stuck out,' I lifted Dot's blue stained mug off the sink; stuck my finger in the air, 'like this. And she wore a diamond; on her little finger, the diamond was the size of a cherry on top of a cherry bakewell.'

'Must've been brilliant,' Dot told the wall behind me, her voice all dreamy, 'like on the Marilyn Monroe films.'

I couldn't keep the fib up for long.

'Only messing, Dot. We shared a curry in Mrs Wong's and drank tap water.'

'You little cow,' she snatched her mug out of my hand. 'I was made up for you then. Still,' she smiled at me, 'suppose a curry's better than nothing, it's a start.'

All morning Dot had one eye on the door and I knew she was waiting for Alex. About twenty past twelve I saw him in the queue. Dot saw him too and smirked at me.

A little girl holding her mother's hand took too long choosing between a jam doughnut and a ring doughnut, so Stella served him.

Dot was furious. 'Let Robyn serve Alex in future when he comes in, Stella.'

'Who's Alex?'

'The good-looking lad from the shop next door; looks a bit like Bryan Ferry.'

'And how am I supposed to do that?'

'Oh, forget it,' Dot said. 'Everything's such a big deal to some people.'

'No, you tell me,' Stella said, hands on hips. 'I'm sure if he wanted Robyn to serve him he'd have made sure she did.'

'Are you trying to say he's avoiding her?'

'Did I say that?'

'Or that he fancies you?'

'It doesn't matter,' I lied, looking towards the door. 'It's no big deal. I don't care if I serve him or not.'

On my dinner, Maud came into the back to see me, 'When do you need to take that week off?'

'I'm going up to the hospital tonight. I'll find out when Nan's coming home. Can I let you know tomorrow?'

'Okay,' Maud said, 'tomorrow at the latest.'

My eyes were sore by the end of the day from watching the door, but he didn't come back in.

'I'll make sure you serve him tomorrow,' Dot said, glaring at Stella, 'stupid arse-licker.'

After work I got the bus to Fazakerley Hospital. Nan was lying down in bed awake. She looked tired but smiled when she saw me, 'I'll be coming home this week. They've been good, the staff in here, but I miss my own place, miss you, love. I worry about you there on your own.'

'I'm all right. Maud says I can take a week off work to help. I have to let her know what days. And Betty's been great. I've given the nurse outside a phone number for the shop, they'll ring me.'

'It could be Friday now the op's over with. Probably best to take next week off. Betty can help until you're home, she's a good 'un. What've you been up to?'

'Nothing.'

'Nothing, don't believe that.'

'I went to Southport, bought a dress and a bag from a second-hand shop. The bag had this Stratton compact thing inside…'

'A Stratton compact?' Nan smiled. 'I had a Stratton compact, had my initials engraved on it. I loved that, loved smartening myself up. Coming out of the Odeon one night, it dropped. Pieces flew in all directions but I picked every one of them up, never did put them back together. Show me once I'm home. I'd like to see that.'

'You can have it, Nan.' I kissed her on the cheek; told her I'd come back tomorrow; standing in the corridor for ages, watching her through the glass panel in the door, she didn't look well, today. She caught me looking, gave me a wave, I waved back.

The next afternoon in work, Maud said she'd like a word. 'Just had a call from the hospital, they're discharging her later on today. You can start your week off from tomorrow.'

She was asleep in bed when I got there, Betty was sipping a cuppa. Even though I enjoyed sleeping in a real bed, it was great to have Nan back.

Betty stood up. 'If you need anything, don't hesitate to knock.'

'Thank you so much.'

'Don't be daft. It's no problem. Keep an eye on her.'

'I will.'

Soon after Betty left, Nan woke up. 'Robyn, love, my mouth's parched.'

'I'll make you a tea.'

Her voice a whisper, 'It's a cold drink I need. Run over the shop for lemonade?'

When I got back her eyes were heavy. 'You all right, Nan?'

'A drink, that's all I need.'

I unscrewed the top of the lemonade bottle, put it to her lips. She took one sip, then another. Her lips were cracked and dry. 'Can I get you anything else?'

She lay back down, closed her eyes. 'Need rest. You always get worse, before you get better.'

Nan slept for a couple of hours. When she finally woke up she didn't look good.

'Sodding pain in my chest,' she said.

I put the lemonade to her lips. She took a sip but it didn't stay down. I ran into the kitchen and fetched the white bowl. Nan coughed up blood and her breath came in fast.

She patted my hand. 'Sorry, love. I'll be better in the morning. Go on, you get some sleep. I'm all right; my body's in shock from the op, that's all. You're a wonderful girl, Robyn, kind, and kindness is important, it'll help draw good people to you.'

Nan was the one person in my life that I could rely on. When I was younger, I'd had nightmares about losing her, the awful empty feeling the next morning. I'd beg Mum to let me go and see her, make sure she was okay.

'Night, Nan. I'll leave the lemonade on the table.'

All night, I couldn't sleep; kept going into her room, checking.

Eight o'clock, I opened the draw curtains to let in some light. It was five past nine when Betty knocked with a pan of scrambled eggs. 'Might give her some energy, is she awake?'

I shook my head.

'Tip this into one of May's pots for later.'

After I'd washed Betty's pan I took it back to her, she was closing the draw curtains.

'Sit down a minute, please, Robyn.'

I gave her the pan back, knelt down by Nan's bed; touched her hand. It was cold.

I looked up at Betty, 'She still asleep Betty?'

She didn't reply.

'Betty?'

Her eyes welled up.

'What's the matter?'

'She's dead, love,' she said, like she was telling me something else. Like the washing's dry, love, or the lecky man's in the next block.

'Must've slipped away in her sleep; not a bad way to go.'

What? Not a bad way to go? What was that supposed to mean? So it was good, then, to slip away without saying you're leaving. No. Nan would not slip anywhere without letting somebody know. Without letting me know. I wanted somebody here who knew what they were talking about.

'Please, get the doctor. She only needs a doctor.'

'She's stone cold, love. I'm so sorry.'

'Stop saying that. You're not a doctor. Get the doctor,' I shook Nan's shoulder; a bit of her silver fringe fell over her eye, gold crucifix the wrong side of her neck. 'Nan, wake up, Nan?' She didn't move. I lifted the green candlewick blanket up to her neck,

'For Christ's sake, Betty, she's freezing. Will you get the doctor or shall I?'

I didn't like to see Nan like that. It all started with the pain in her hip; then she stopped eating very much, sent me to the shop for more pain killers. Different ones each time. 'Your body stops responding,' she said, 'can't keep feeding it the same thing.' And she hadn't got her teeth in. Her mouth was shrunken, lips disappearing, as if death, in a sneaky way, grabbed one bit at a time, and said, no more singing for you, May; no going the club for you, drinking Guinness.

After Betty had left, I kept tight hold of Nan's hand. Her beautiful silver fringe flicked out at the edges. And the look on her face, like everything she needed to do had been completed. I begged her to hold on a little bit longer, 'Betty's gone for the doctor. She'll be back now. Don't go yet, please, Nan, not yet, I need to tell you something, something important, about a lad. And you haven't finished your lemonade.'

7

Mum came out of Nan's bedroom, walking towards me. I hadn't seen her for two years, she walked right past, into the kitchen. 'Awful time for this to happen, Owen's mad busy in the pub and one of his barmaids has gone off to have her baby.' She shuffled things around in kitchen drawers, clicked open Nan's black handbag; walked her fingers across papers; took something with Co-op Insurance written on the front. 'You want her cross and chain?'

'I don't want anything.' Mum's eyes were red from crying. 'At least she'll be with Jack, eh?' She flapped a hanky from a pocket, blew her nose.

I thought about what Nan said, about looking her best for Grandad. I found the little Stratton compact; handed it to Mum. 'It was for Nan, but–'

She dropped it in her pocket. 'I'll make sure she gets it before she leaves. She hated hospitals and doctors. They've let her out too early by the sound of it. How was she when she came home?'

'Tired, her voice was shaky, and her lips were all cracked.'

'Thought so, you're just a number in those places.'

'Nan said they took good care of her.'

'You'll have to come and live in Edinburgh after the funeral, do a few little shifts for us in the pub to pay your keep.'

'No!' I said.

Mum wasn't listening to me. 'Poor May, still living in the dark ages. She hasn't even got a telly. Look at all these stupid books, gathering dust. What a waste of money.'

'We have a radio, love books, we talk, tell stories, we don't need a telly.'

I picked up a ball of Nan's wool, it felt soft and warm in my hands. 'I won't be going to Edinburgh, I've got plans.'

'You've got nowhere to live. These places are for pensioners. There's a small box room…'

'Will you listen? I'm not leaving Liverpool, my job, my mates, I'm not twelve anymore, you can't tell me what to do.'

'Staying here for what, some crummy job in a bakery with buttons for wages? And where're you gonna live? What's wrong with Edinburgh and what's wrong with me and Owen?'

Everything, I thought. For starters she wasn't even looking me in the eye when she spoke. There was no way she wanted a teenage kid going back to Edinburgh with her. 'Erm, thanks for that, but Rose's mum said I can live with them,' I lied.

'She got enough room? Hasn't Rose got a sister? Well, you've left school now, that's up to you. Let me know before this time next week.'

It was the night before Nan's funeral; Mum asked me for my front door key, was handing them back to the housing before she left. 'Young girl like you shouldn't be living with a pensioner, anyway,' Mum said. 'Wait till you move into Rose's house. You won't know you're born.'

But I haven't given you my answer, yet, I wanted to say. And I've changed my mind. I am coming to Edinburgh after all, to see the look on Mum's face. I didn't know where I was going to live, even thought about asking Rose but she slept in their tiny box room, her mum and dad had the bigger front bedroom, Rita slept on a settee now, refusing to share a room with Rose. They murdered each other.

'She's the last to go, your nan, lost her brothers and sisters years ago. Bridie was before her, went a few years ago. She was a nark, younger than May, but a miserable woman with three miserable kids; don't want any of them at the funeral, on the hunt for butties and sausage rolls. Only come out the woodwork if something's fuckin' free.'

Mum knocked Nan's tablets by accident and they clattered to the floor. She picked them up, tossed them onto the sideboard. 'One of the eldest, Mam, and she outlived them all.'

'Betty upstairs was good to Nan,' I said, 'and good to me.'

'All right, tomorrow, after the funeral, we'll take Betty across the road to the club for a few drinks, okay?'

I nodded.

'The rest of them can fuck off.'

Inside the kitchen, away from Mum, I sipped my cup of tea. On the worktop, the little cake tray Nan had got me, when I was eleven; gave me money so I could buy ingredients to make coconut pyramids. Nan who sang old songs, like: *Hey, Good Lookin'*, who cooked lamb chops every Sunday, went down the Pier Head to walk it off and feed the birds: who had memories and stories I never knew, would probably now, never know.

Mum needn't have worried, nobody came to the funeral, just me,

Mum and Betty. There were a few women scattered across the benches. They sang hymns and joined in the mass. The priest talked about Nan with dressed-up words, tried to play down the fact that he was talking about a stranger. Betty sat right at the back: Mum sat on the first bench, in front of Nan's coffin without saying a word. Both of us, dressed all in black sitting right next to each other. This is what being on your own feels like, I thought. And it felt shitty.

Somebody rang a little bell, I stared at the coffin, saw Nan's life growing strong again, lifting itself up towards the high colourful windows. The dull morning light shifted inside the church in an extraordinary way. It was as though the light had captured the room, lifting it back in time, to the evening when Nan first met Grandad Jack.

In a few seconds, everything was changed into something squashed and unrecognisable. Then it was gone, in an awful hurry, the end of something wonderful slipped out of the stained-glass window without too much fuss, like it had somewhere more important to be.

I pictured Nan sitting in a red velvet seat at the Odeon on London Road, on the back row; holding hands with her Jack. May, all done up in her best sage-green crepe frock, and pressed-powdered face; peach lippy, Stratton compact in her bag. The warming of old promises stirring once again in their minds.

One time there were three of us. Now it was just me and Mum, who was probably thinking about escaping Liverpool, and getting back to Edinburgh. I spent the quiet time in mass, and later, at the cemetery, trying to come up with a plan.

"*What's on your mind?*" Nan would've asked if she was here.

"*Remember, Robyn, don't rely on anybody but yourself.*"

The thought of always having to rely on me made my breaths

come in small. There was no way I could be that strong. But the truth was, with everything opening up around me, I didn't have any choice.

That night, we walked to the club opposite Nan's. Mum went straight to the bar. The man with the red moustache was serving.
 'Sorry about May, girl,' he said to me. 'We'll miss her in here.'
 'What do you want?' Mum asked.
 'Orange juice,' I said.
 'Vodka and orange and one orange juice, mate.'
 'I thought you drank cider,' I said.
 'I do. Make sure the vodka's a double.'
 About half an hour later, Betty came in with her husband, Larry. Then another couple, Ada and John came in and joined us. Mum filled the table with drinks for them then sat back down. It was Friday night, there was a singer on playing a guitar. Mum and Larry drank two drinks to everyone else's one. Larry got the spoons out, clattered them along to *Singin' the Blues*. Ada and Betty sang, Mum took vodka from her bag, tipped it into her glass and drank.
 A drunken man asked her to dance. She fixed her eyes on him, took a gulp of her drink; told him to piss off.
 'Is that how you speak to someone who's asked you nicely to dance?'
 'Sit down, Joey.' Betty said. 'She's buried her mam today.'
 Mum spoke to Betty. 'Buried me mam or not, I wouldn't dance with the likes of that lowlife if you paid me.'
 'Listen to the lady of the manor over there, Joey Muldoon doesn't ask a lady twice. Not that you are a lady. That was my mistake.' He burped then walked away.

'Gobshite,' Mum said; stabbing his back with her eyes.

'You all right, Robyn?' Betty said. 'Been a rough few days for you, love. Going to stay with your mum in Edinburgh?'

'No, my friend says I can stay at her house.'

Joey Muldoon was being told he'd had enough to drink, and he wasn't getting served any more. Joey swung a punch at the man behind the bar; it landed with a *boof*, just below his eye. Two other customers grabbed Joey by the arms and ran him out through the double doors.

'I've offered,' Mum said, 'told her she can serve behind the bar in the foot hospital. But no,' she looked at me, eyes flickering under the strip lights, head cocked to the side, 'knows it all, don't yer? Thinks she'll find something better. Won't leave her mates or her crummy job,' she took another sip of her drink. 'You can't force them.'

'No,' Betty said. 'You can't.'

Larry started up on the spoons again.

'For Christ's sake,' Mum said to Larry, 'enough on those stupid spoons, you've got my head fucking banging over here.'

Larry looked at John and they both burst out laughing. Larry lifted the glass of mild up to his lips. Mum flattened her cigarette into the ashtray, got up to go the toilet, jabbed Larry's shoulder with her elbow as she pushed past. Larry nearly choked, spat the ale all over his jacket; slammed the glass down on the table. His face was red with laughing. 'Wouldn't like to bring a short week home to her,' he said, scratching the back of his head. 'Sod that for a game of soldiers.'

Ada and Betty sat close and said nothing. My mouth felt dry. I picked Mum's vodka up and drank it down. It hit the back of my throat first, then it was in my belly, but the warm fuzzy feeling I got in my chest felt great. I pushed my orange juice over by her ashtray; picked at the red fake velvet seat. 'Bet you've never had a dull moment living with her,' Larry said to me. 'She's a case.'

The vodka made me relax a little, my brain felt like it was working a bit slower, a feeling I liked.

'She's a laugh a minute,' I said, 'splits your guts wide open.'

Sometimes, when I remembered the past, and how me and my mum spent years trying to avoid getting battered, avoid being killed, and how many chances she gave him, I think in my head I must have made it up. Snatched it somehow out of my imagination, let it dance itself into existence at the centre of my mind. After a few days in my mother's company, I realised it was real. And I understood the importance of forgetting.

Betty rested her hand on my hand. 'May was a good soul, loved you to bits, she knew something not many people find out,' she glanced across at Mum, coming out of the toilets. 'Life's much more than just thinking about yourself.'

Larry got another round in, carried the drinks back over on a square tray. Before Mum came back I swapped her vodka and orange for my orange juice. When I saw her crossing the room, I downed it in three goes. Betty gave me a sly smile, glanced straight ahead again.

A couple of people got up and gave a song. Everybody just getting merry and singing along to old songs I wasn't supposed to know. When I sang along Betty laughed and nudged Ada. 'Listen to this one, knows all the words to, *Settin' the Woods on Fire.*'

Mum tasted her drink, smelt it; looked over at the barman and made her eyes small. 'Tight-arsed little shit: I could spit more,' took the bottle of vodka out of her bag and tipped loads into the glass.

'Any more singers?' the man with the guitar asked.

I stood up, he handed me the microphone. 'What're you singing love?'

Nan had a favourite song she loved, '*Mack the Knife.*'

When I'd finished singing I gave the microphone back to the man. 'Thanks, my nan, May, loved that song.'

'Ahh, ladies and gentlemen, the young lady sang that for May. Let's hear it for her.'

I heard people clapping; sat down and Mum tutted at me. 'Mack the knife?' she twisted the cap off the last of her vodka, 'Mack the fucking knife? She wasn't an underworld cut-throat, for Christ's sake, she was a cleaner.'

'So what?' I said.

'Don't so what me you cheeky cow.'

'What did you want me to sing? *Do You Want Your Old Lobby Washed Down, Con Shine*?'

'You being funny?'

Larry said to Mum, 'She's got a good voice, she get that from you?'

'No, she gets it from her useless, runaway fath-'

She caught herself and stopped.

Ada said, 'A small rendition of *My Bonnie Lies Over the Ocean* always goes down well on such occasions as funerals.'

Betty said, 'That's a nice one, that, Ada, My Bonnie.'

Mum said, 'She was Irish you daft cow; not Scottish.'

Larry said, 'Does it matter? *Bonnie Lies Over the Ocean* is a good song. And everyone knows the words.'

John grinned at Mum, '*Lemon Squeezer* by The Four Barons.'

Mum flung her eyes to the ceiling; glared at me as if to say, look what you've started now.

Larry carried on. '*Peas and Rice*, Eddie Cleanhead Vinson.'

Betty shot him with her eyes. 'Shut it, Larry.'

'*Keep Your Hands On Your...*'

Betty slapped Larry's arm with the back of her hand. 'Now pack it in, you should be ashamed in front of a young girl.'

Larry looked shocked, 'I'm not making them up. Tiny Bradshaw sang *Keep Your Hands on Your...*'

'I'm warning you,' Betty said.

'He did not,' John shouted. 'Bullmoose Jackson sang that.'

Ada told John to button his lip.

Larry stood, pointed a finger right in John's face. 'You're wrong, sonny Jim. Bullmoose Jackson sang, *Big Fat Mammas Are Back in Style.*'

Mum looked at Ada and Betty; spat her vodka all over the table. She howled laughing.

'Last song then, *Beer Bottle Boogie*,' the man with the guitar announced, 'Johnny Otis.'

And everyone in the club stole sly looks at the table in the corner, full of laughing mourners.

'May would've loved tonight,' Betty said, 'with all the shenanigans.'

'Yeah, shame she's dead,' Mum said. My nan is far from dead, I thought.

Once everyone began leaving to go home, I checked my coat, felt inside the empty pocket where the door key used to be, longing for something solid to hold onto.

8

Behind a bush in Nan's front garden were four carrier bags full of clothes. I'd told Mum they were in a wardrobe in Rose's bedroom. I thought about saying, I have been to a nightclub and drank cider and fancy someone who works in Man's Gear. And I have no place to sleep tonight, but changed my mind.

Before she got on the bus to Lime Street, Mum said,

'You'll be all right, always are. Fall down the toilet and come back up smelling like flowers.'

'You mean roses?'

'Roses, flowers, what's the difference?'

Her saying this pissed me off; part of me felt like screaming at her, she really didn't know anything about me, hadn't even made an effort to try and find out. 'There's a big difference,' I said, 'not all of them have thorns.'

I watched the bus pull away. She sat downstairs, looked out of the back window and waved. I was sixteen. I had nowhere to live. I was waving my mother off on the bus, knowing I'd probably never see her again.

And I felt like a terrible daughter because I was glad.

I always had to have a plan. Like last night in the club. You never knew what Mum would do next and that scared me. My plan was to keep myself out of my mother's world. That's what I'd done. That's why, once the bus was completely out of sight, and I knew she'd really gone, it sounded mad, but I felt a little bit better about everything.

One of the first things I had to do was to find my dad, hopefully he was still alive. Even if he wanted nothing to do with me, at least I'd know and could let go of this longing.

Behind me, the doors of St Anthony's church were open. It was pointless going to get my clothes. Thank God it wasn't raining or they'd have got soaked. I stepped inside, dipped my finger into the holy water and blessed myself, sat down on one of the back benches.

The church was empty. I looked at the place beneath the altar, where Nan's coffin had rested. There was only one lady polishing brasses and stacking up blue floppy hymn books. When she saw me she made her way over.

'You all right, love?'

'Yeah, thanks.'

'Not in work?'

'I'm going in now.'

'Your nan wasn't it, the other day?'

I nodded.

'Ahh, sorry love, you're lucky though, to have a job, two million unemployed. It was on the news. And these schemes, waste of time; there's no jobs at the end. It pays buttons, slave labour. You're not on a scheme are you?'

'Yeah.'

'Look somewhere else. There'll be nothing at the end of it.'

'It doesn't matter. It'll do me for now.'

'Some place where they'll keep you on. That's what I've told my grandson, those schemes are worthless.'

But she was wrong. I had met new people, was learning new things every day, had a job I liked, and that wasn't nothing, that was something; something to tell people about when I was interviewed again. Then they'd know I'd worked, they'd see I hadn't been wasting my time, and there'd be a reference at the end. It would give me a better chance than somebody who'd done nothing.

Walking out of church without Nan, I felt like one of those worn cracks in the pavement, dark, thin and uneven, good for holding nothing.

I caught the bus, made my way to Waterford's. Could see Dot through the window, thought about going in, but changed my mind, walked down to the Walker Gallery, sat inside until closing.

That night, I lay down on a bench in St John's Gardens. There was a group of people by the railings, smoking, and drinking ale, three men and one woman. The woman came over with a flask, poured a cup of milky tea, handed it to me. I thanked her, drank it down, 'Take care of yourself,' she said. Then she was gone.

The following night, I went back to the same place, hoping to see the woman who gave me the tea, to talk to her, get some advice, but she wasn't around. I went back to the same bench, hoping she'd pass by. The last thing I remembered before falling asleep, was hearing someone singing a song I didn't know, in between coughing his guts up.

It was a man who woke me, I thought, or the rain falling on my face. He wore huge dark boots beneath his black coat. He stank of piss and ale. Under a street light, I could see his fingernails were filthy. He poked my arm. 'Pigs over there,' he said, 'better move or they'll catch you; got a fag?'

I sat up, 'Thanks,' I said, 'I don't smoke.'

'Follow me, this way,' then he sang, '*I know a place, far away from the crowds.*'

Half asleep, I started to follow him out of the gardens. We hadn't got far when I changed my mind, turned to cross over, felt a hand grab me by the back of the neck. He pushed me forwards up some steps and into the bushes, covered my mouth with a filthy palm before I could scream. He was strong, so strong my feet were no longer touching the ground. His palm covered my nose, I was struggling to breathe, tried to kick him but my legs wouldn't move. I could hear his wet cough.

'Me an' you gonna have a little party,' he said.

I tried wriggling out of his grasp, which made him laugh. 'You're not going anywhere, Missy,' he said. I saw spit dribbling from his mouth, like a neighbour's dog from years ago, felt his rough lips sucking on my ear, his awful tongue tasting my skin. 'I bet you're still new,' he whispered.

He threw me down onto the ground. I banged my back on the trunk of a tree, screamed out in pain. He knelt; pulled up the hem on my tweed coat, I tried to push it back down, he let go, picked up a brick with one hand, fumbled with the zip on his trousers with the other. He raised the brick, 'You scream once more, Missy, an' I'll cave yer fuckin' head in.'

He pushed aside his thick, black coat, breathing fast, caught his zip and moaned. I took a chance and leapt up, tried to run, was too slow; he grabbed the back of my hair, lifted the brick up high above my head. I pushed my elbow out hard backwards; caught him between the legs, heard him cry out, for a second he let go of me. I ran, fast against the wind, up towards the Adelphi, too frightened to look back.

Breathless by the time I got there; trying hard to swallow the sobs that wouldn't stop coming. It was half five in the morning when I got to the shop, another couple of hours before it opened. The streets were deserted, no cars on the roads. A milk cart rattled down Mount Pleasant, the driver stopped at Waterford's, left a pint of milk on the step and drove away.

I needed a drink, sat on Waterford's step, pushed my thumb through the crimson top on the milk and swigged, trying to stop my hands trembling, to keep down the panic that was still rising. The pissy smell of his thick coat crawling on my skin.

A few minutes before the shop opened, I walked to the top of Mount Pleasant, waited until Dot opened up, gave it another ten minutes then straightened myself out, made my way back down the road.

Dot smiled when she saw me. 'Hiya, Robyn. Come here.' She hugged me into her chest. Her overall smelled lovely, icing and Charlie perfume. She caught me wincing.

'You okay?'

'Yeah just banged my back a bit.'

'You're freezing. I'll make us a cuppa. Sorry to hear about your nan. What brings you into work so soon?'

'I just got on the bus. Where's Maud?'

'Gone to buy milk, some bugger drank ours,' she held up the empty bottle.

I looked away.

'You okay?'

'Yes.'

I don't know why people say they're okay when they're not. Nan even said she was okay that night before she died. I wondered what Dot would do if I said, no, I'm not okay, I'm scared. I'm saying I'm okay because it's easier. It's much easier than letting this hurt break open.

Nan didn't want to upset me; that was why she said she felt okay. And maybe she thought that saying it meant she would be. Hurrying into the back of the shop, scrubbing my hands and face in the sink with soap, the water blended in with the tears. I was tired, the back of my head and my back throbbed.

From the front of the shop, I heard a man's voice, 'That young minx who works here in yet?'

'You mean Robyn?' Dot said.

'That's her.'

'She's in the back, why?'

'I'll tell you why, drank your milk earlier, seen her with my own eyes.'

Silence.

Dot said, 'She told me she drank it, gave me the money for it in fact, so you need to keep your fat gob shut.'

'Take it easy, as long as you didn't think I delivered it in that condition.'

'What's going on, Robyn?' Dot asked after the milkman had left.

'Nothing.'

Stella opened the door, pushed past us, through the passageway and into the toilet.

'Robyn?' Dot said.

I didn't know what to say, walked out onto the shop floor, felt glad that for the next eight hours at least, I would be warm and safe.

9

We were busy, a group of American tourists came in all at once; the queue stretched past Man's Gear and the Wimpy, they were staying at the Adelphi. I liked the way they spoke, calling jam doughnuts jelly doughnuts: that made me smile.

On our dinner, Dot said, 'I'm sorry, love. Last thing you need is me going on at you, but if I can be of any help…'

'Thanks, Dot.'

Stella and Maud were careful around me, smiling more than usual asking if I was okay. Stella even touched my arm, and said, 'Sorry to hear about your awful news.'

Maud said, 'If you need to go early just let me know.'

I thanked Maud, told her it was better for me to keep busy. She nodded and gave me an extra ten minutes on my morning break with Dot. It felt good being around so much kindness; I saw Nan everywhere, women who came in wearing head scarves, ordering her favourite, a packet of fruit scones. I worried about the things I hadn't said, realised how lucky I was to have always had Nan's place to go back to.

'It's a shame,' Dot said, 'your nan leaving while you're still so young. I lost my nan when I was nineteen. She was the love of my life, let me get away with murder.'

She started filling up, and so did I, but I didn't want her to see me; didn't want to cry here. I excused myself and sat on the lid of the toilet. Waterford's staff couldn't find out about me being homeless. I'd get the sack; have to leave without a reference, end up with nothing, which would make it harder for me to get another job. I had to find a safe place to sleep.

10

The day disappeared before I knew it, Maud was cashing up the till. After we'd closed, I made my way to the Odeon on London Road, watched a film about two men who sang and danced dressed as woodpeckers, and were framed for a bank robbery, they ended up in jail. One of them freaked out, and everybody started laughing, including me, forgetting about Nan for a bit, and the fact that I had nowhere to live.

After the film had finished, I walked down to Waterford's and curled up on the step. My clothes were still in the bushes at Nan's place. Eventually, I dropped off into a half-sleep.

The woman who woke me was about the same age as Stella, maybe twenty, 'You okay?' she asked.
'Yeah.'
'Don't tell me you plan on sleeping here all night?'
'What's it to you?'
'Had an argument with your mum and dad?'
'Yeah,' I said, so she wouldn't ask any more questions.

She wore black trousers, with a silver low-necked top; her hair was brown, curly, shoulder-length, she wore a thick silver charm bracelet on her wrist, it jangled when she moved.

'Thought so.'

'What time is it?'

'Nearly half one; I'm not leaving you here,' she said, 'wouldn't be able to sleep. I have a flat a few minutes away, you could sleep on my settee?'

'I'm okay, going home now.'

'Police come they'll lock you in a cell. My settee is better than a cell, or that cold step.'

'I said I'm okay.'

'Look, come and see, if you don't like my place, you can leave. I'll make you a hot drink and a sandwich; it's warm?'

She had this rich smoky smell about her, like nothing I'd experienced before. I could tell by her eyes she'd been drinking, but she seemed okay, had a nice smile. My back was still sore and freezing cold. I supposed a hot drink and a something to eat would make me feel better. To be warm, just for a couple of hours, maybe get a wash in her bathroom, would be something.

Her flat was a ten minute walk away, on top of a jeweller's shop on Bold Street. I sat on the settee and it was okay. There was a beautiful oblong cream rug in the centre, a rocking chair next to the lecky fire, with red velvet cushions. Pictures of butterflies and elephants all over the walls, a large plant in the corner with thin, pointy leaves; the tall lamps gave off a soft orange light, made me feel warm. It was the fact that it was tucked away, hidden up a narrow flight of stairs, that I didn't like, not having your own front door leading directly to the street, made it all feel false somehow.

Her face appeared around the door, 'Cheese or ham?'

'Thanks, cheese is good.'
'What's your name?'
'Robyn.'
'I'm Terri.'

After I'd eaten, we sat and chatted for a while. She took off her clothes, sat next to me wearing just her black knickers and bra, took a tin out from under the settee; lit an already rolled cigarette that smelled the same as she did. She offered some of it to me; I shook my head.

'Drink, then?' she said.

I thought about how much I needed to get some sleep, how, in the club, drinking Mum's vodka relaxed me.

'You have any vodka?'

She came back with a vodka and orange filled up to the top in a pint glass. Carried on taking drags from her cigarette, head flung backwards resting against the top of the settee, blowing smoke up to the yellow ceiling. I sipped the vodka, felt my body begin to relax.

'Knock it back, angel face, it'll help you sleep.'

I took a big gulp, felt it hit my throat, warming my chest. It felt good. I kept sipping but didn't drink it all, maybe half.

'Lose some layers,' she said, 'you're gonna need all the help you can get, that settee is uncomfortable as hell.'

'I'm all right,' I said.

She put a record on, the intro made me feel lonesome, a powerful saxophone sound, or maybe a trumpet, then the voice singing a sad, but hopeful song about transformation, and finding a home, all of the things I was searching for.

I slipped out of my shoes, pulled my socks off.

'Gerry fucking Rafferty,' Terri said.

I loved the song, listened to it over and over, stood up to put it on again and knocked the rest of my drink all over the rug. 'Oh god, I'm so sorry.'

Terri shrugged. 'It's okay, I can get it cleaned. No harm done.'

She stood up, began to dance, her eyes all glittery, she held both of my hands and we danced and danced and danced, the rug felt soft and warm beneath my soles. We danced until we had no energy left.

Exhausted, we fell onto the settee, she flung her head back; her eyes were closed now when she spoke her speech slow and slurry, 'I don't know why life turns shitty on us, but you can't let it push you into the passenger seat, you have to drive your own vehicle, learn how to fix it when it fuckin' fails, and it always fuckin' fails.'

I was tired, couldn't wait for her to go to bed, tried hard to keep my eyes open. 'You do favours for people in life, Robyn, you get rewards: loads and loads of rewards. Did you know that?' She chatted on about her brother, how she missed him now he'd moved, then she stopped, looked at me. 'You know you're really pretty,' she said. 'My brother has a modelling agency, in Manchester. You mind if I take a few photos of you and post them to him? It'll mean paid work, you have a job?'

'No,' I lied, suddenly not wanting her to know anything about me. 'I don't.'

'Great, there's plenty of work in Manchester. Last young girl I got work, ended up posing on sheepskin rugs, brilliant pics; clothes on, she's been signed by an agent for a film.'

I didn't like the sound of being photographed on a sheepskin rug, or Manchester. I felt sick, wanted to leave. She took a black square bag from a cupboard in the corner, lifted out a huge camera. Then I thought she might be telling the truth, but wondered why she was roaming the streets at that hour on her own? Why wasn't her brother getting her jobs in Manchester? She was pretty, well nicer-looking than me.

I wanted to run right back down those narrow stairs; tried to think of something to say to make her leave the room, to stop her taking pictures. 'Sorry, don't look my best, can we do the photos tomorrow, after I've tidied myself up?'

She stood staring at me, lips thin and harsh now. Then she put on that smile again, the one outside the bakery, slid the camera back in its case, left it by the chair. 'Of course, great idea, tomorrow it is, here's a blanket. Need some sleep myself, we can talk more tomorrow when we're both fresh?'

'Okay, night.'

'Night; angel face.'

I heard her lock the main door, covered myself with the blanket, pretended to sleep; heard her room door click shut. Sitting up, staring at the camera case for ages, when I thought she might have dozed off, I got up, unfastened the clasp and opened the black lid.

11

I was rummaging around in the case then she came out of her room, padded into the bathroom. Slamming the case shut, I fell backwards, crawled towards the settee and lay back down. In the doorway, she stood, naked, toothbrush sticking out of the side of her mouth. She made her way over to the settee, so near I could smell mint and the funny smoke on her breath.

'My brother will be made up with you,' she pointed the brush at me, 'the pics will be brilliant, he's got a brand new car, black leather seats.'

I tried to keep my voice smooth, 'Really? Brilliant, can't wait to meet him. Night, see you tomorrow.'

'He bought me one; not as good as his. I'll take you for a drive tomorrow if you like?'

'Sounds good,' I lied.

'You're gonna love Manchester, meet the others, make new friends. He will love your pics, you have good skin.'

Half an hour I gave it, unlocked her front door, tiptoed down the stairs and out through the main door.

I ran all the way back up to Waterford's. Crouched in a corner of the doorway; it wasn't long before I was shivering again. Knees up to my chin, eyes wide open. This time I didn't fall asleep, it wasn't safe to. I was glad to be away from Terri, didn't trust her and never wanted to cross paths with her again. To keep myself awake, I hummed, *Mack the Knife*.

12

'Where did you sleep last night?' Dot said. 'You look terrible, look in the mirror at your hair. You've got huge bags under your eyes, and don't lie to me, Robyn.'

I looked in the mirror. She was right.

'Robyn?'

'What? I stayed in Rose's, she had a party. I was up late.'

I hated lying.

'You can say that again. Clean yourself up before Maud sees you. Look at the colour of your fingernails. You can't serve food like that.'

I took the soap and scrubbed my hands, felt weak, my bones slow and heavy, was unsure how I would get through the day.

Alex came in at lunchtime. I went to the toilet, didn't want to talk to him, dreading night-time coming, feeling edgy and tearful and dying to scream. I had no idea such an awful side of life existed on the streets, thought about ringing Mum in the pub, but that would be taking a step backwards. I had to find a place to live, but how? My wages weren't enough to pay rent on a place. I had to think things through, to clear my head, find a way to live life better than this. Things would work out, something would come along. I closed my eyes, imagined myself back in Nan's, soaking in a tub of hot water, bubbles soft beneath my chin. The big white towels that wrapped around you like a hug, and lovely Nan, waiting for the sound of my key scraping the lock.

After work I went to Rose's. I'd been putting it off, telling her. I didn't know why. Having to own up to being homeless or something, probably, like I'd failed at life already. Her mum and dad were in the local pub at a friend's funeral.

'Stay here tonight, have a warm bath. They'll be that pissed when they get back they won't know.' Rita had gone the pictures with her mate. Rose had the place to herself. She hugged me tight, said it'd be fun to have me staying over.

'Are you all right?' she asked. 'Really, I mean, I know how much you loved May. I'm so very, very sorry, Robyn. Where will you live? I can ask my parents?'

Out of nowhere they came, the tears that turned into sobs, that flooded down my face hot and soft, I didn't even try to wipe them away.

13

The next day, in work, I felt so much better, my body was clean; my clothes had all been washed. Rose lent me a pair of faded Levi's, a sweatshirt and underwear until mine were dry. Dot smiled when she saw me. 'That's more like it,' she said.

Rose told me she would ask her mum today if I could stay in her house for a bit, until I got myself sorted. What a difference one night made, my future was looking better. I put the idea of contacting Mum right out of my head.

Later that afternoon, Rose rang the shop, said her grandad had had a fall, and was staying with them until he got better. She'd asked her mum and dad about me, but they said now wasn't a good time. I told her not to worry, I'd find somewhere.

When the shop closed, I walked up to London Road. Behind me, heard a familiar jangling sound I couldn't quite place, turned around to see Terri.

'Hiya, angel face,' she said, waving, the jingle of her charm bracelet now loud in my ears.

'Oh, hiya,' I said, but carried on walking.

'Slow down. Not nice disappearing without even a tarra?'

'Sorry, I had to leave in a hurry.'

She caught up with me, linked her arm through mine, I thought of Nan.

'Emergency was it? Had to get to Waterford's for your shift?'

'I don't work in…'

'Liar, I walked past this afternoon, saw you stacking pasties all nice and neat inside the oven.'

I felt sick.

'There's a favour or two owed, I think, don't you? Wouldn't want the staff in there finding out you're homeless, reeking of God knows what, scabbed-up around food? Not brilliant for their reputation is it? Management wouldn't like that at all.'

'What do you want?' I snapped.

She stopped outside a café. 'Come in here for a cuppa and we'll talk.'

Terri didn't ask me what I'd like, but ordered a pot of tea for two, and two toasted teacakes. I watched her pour the tea, spread butter onto a teacake and eat.

'Tuck in,' she said.

I shook my head.

'Suit yourself.' She drank all of the tea, ate both teacakes, swung back on her chair. 'Let's carry on where we left off, shall we? I would like to take a few photographs of you to send to my brother. Maybe tonight. It would mean good wages if he can get you work?'

'Whatever,' I said.

'You don't sound too keen?'

If I lost my job, what would be left? That was the most important thing to me right now. I had no choice but to do the stupid bloody photographs, then leg it out of there.

'How long will it take?'

'An hour tops.'

'Okay, after an hour I'm gone.'

'Good,' she clapped her hands too loud; a few people looked over at us. She smiled, whispered, 'My place, seven tonight, I have some vodka left?'

I walked around town. Felt like one door after another was closing in my face. Watched people rushing for buses, nipping into the pub for a pint, holding hands with someone they loved, and me, not feeling part of anything. I could end up ringing Mum and hate myself, give up my independence for safety? No, I wasn't giving up yet, there must be a way to hold onto both.

At seven o'clock, Terri buzzed me in. Not one person knew where I was, I thought, she could kill me, her and whoever else was in there, and they'd never know where to begin looking for my body. I climbed the narrow staircase, dreading what was waiting for me behind her front door.

14

She reached under the settee, took one of her funny cigarettes from the tin. Lit the match, coaxed the end of it into life. I could smell the stink of a dead match, blending with a waft of curry sauce, maybe on low in the oven for her tea, and a cup of fresh coffee on the table. Her camera was already out of the box, on the settee. At least there was nobody else in the flat, nobody I could see.

'Wanna drink?' she asked.

'No, I'm okay.'

'You don't look okay, you look a little tense?'

'I'm fine.'

'A shot of vodka will help you relax; the camera is kinder to a relaxed face.'

The mingling of the smells was making my stomach feel all floaty.

'Could you open a window?' I asked.

'Sure, take a seat.'

'What do you want me to do?'

She pushed the window open, offered me her cigarette. 'At least have a couple of pulls.'

'I don't want anything, okay, let's get this over with.'

She flopped down into the chair. 'Erm, it might be better if you're wearing a teeny bit less.'

'What?'

'You know, maybe just undies?'

'No.'

'I thought we had a deal?'

I pretended I wasn't feeling scared and uncomfortable. To help me, inside my head I imagined being Rose, fearless and bold. 'You didn't say anything about clothes off in the cafe?'

'It's just, this type of modelling, catalogues, magazines, they're looking for underwear models, that's where the money is.'

'I'm not bothered about the money.'

'But you're bothered about keeping your job, right? But not just that, look, I'm saving you from the stupid, mundane work you're in. God knows we all chose the bottom rung to begin with. Ugly work, serving the public, all the while your life is fuckin' screaming at you: *Haven't you forgotten something?*'

Smoke curled out of her mouth, floated up towards the ceiling, thick and heavy. 'Get a nice nine-to-five we're told at school, become a typist, sit in a stuffy office all day, or go on the factory floor. What we're not told, is eventually, it'll squeeze every ounce of joy out of every fuckin' day, until you die, like me da.'

I had to get out of here fast, was wearing a sweatshirt and jeans, slipped off my shoes, undone my button, pulled the zip down.

Terri smiled, began getting her camera ready. 'Okay, now we can have some fun.'

People were laughing, loud, passing by the window. Someone was screeching, 'No way, that would horrify me.'

Nan came into my mind, asking me about how I wanted

to live my life. I replayed it all, the way I'd sounded, so sure of myself, living the life you imagined was much harder than simply saying the words, especially when your life didn't feel like it was yours anymore.

Without regrets, or something like that I'd answered, or was it without mistakes? That would be my best life. It made me think, this would probably be something I'd regret, something to worry about. I could easily get out of a job I didn't like, but getting out of this, being controlled by a stranger who knew where I worked, that would be something else. Nan would be horrified.

Slipping my shoes back on, I zipped up my jeans, fastened the button and stood up.

Terri looked flabbergasted. 'What're you doing?'

I didn't answer.

She stood, walked over to me. 'I said…'

'I know what you said.'

She made her eyes small. 'Then what the fuck are you doing?'

'What does it look like I'm doing?'

'You said you would…'

'I've changed my mind.'

'What does that mean?'

'I don't have to explain myself to you.'

'I've promised my brother.'

'That's your problem.'

She grabbed hold of my arm. 'Oh, no, I'm not taking the blame for you changing your mind, bitch. You don't understand he'll go fuckin' mental.'

I pulled myself free, made my way to the door; she lunged at me, grabbed hold of my hair. 'My problem, is it, don't fuckin' think so. You owe me. Watch tomorrow when I turn up at your work.'

Twisting out of her grasp, grabbing the camera from her hand, I ran to the window, looked out, nobody around. I let it fall, watched as it smashed into pieces on the pavement. Before she could come at me again, I ran at her, punched her hard in the face, twice.

She fell backwards against the wall, moaning. 'You wait you fuckin' idiot, I'll get you the sack.'

'Do what you like,' I shouted, opening the door, 'by the time you show up they'll already know about me, because I'll have told them myself. And you're the fuckin' bitch.'

I slammed my fist against her door. 'Twisted you are, and I'm sure you can explain to the police why you're keen on taking photographs of girls in their underwear. They'll be crawling all over this place soon.'

'You're fuckin' deeeeeeaaaaad!' she screeched after me.

Outside, I ran all the way to the bus stop on London Road, jumped on the first one that came. Sitting at the back, alone, gazing out of the window I smiled, my whole body felt like it was glistening. Terri didn't know it, but she had woken something up in me. I felt no fear, no anxiety, no having to do things I didn't want to, anymore. Taking a deep breath into my already clear mind, it had all clicked into place, tomorrow, first thing when I got into Waterford's, whether they sacked me or not, I knew what I had to do.

15

'Good grief, you look like a hunter-gatherer.'

'That's because I slept in a doorway.'

'What?' Dot clutched her throat.

'I was okay, the doorway of a small social club, out of the way.'

Stella arrived, jiggled out of her coat.

Dot ignored Stella. 'Robyn, you could have been-'

'I was fine.'

'Give me your mum's number.'

'No, Dot, I don't want to-'

'Don't, no Dot, me. So you'd rather sleep on the streets?'

'Who's on the streets?' Stella said, lifting the overall from her bag.

'This lunatic is; in bleeding doorways.'

Stella fastened up her buttons, said, 'I've got an empty room if you want it, just a box room.'

Dot smirked at Stella, 'Nice time this is to be messing about with jokes. She's serious, you know.'

'Shut it, Dot,' Stella said, smoothing out the creases. She looked at me. 'You want the room or not?'

I looked at Dot, didn't want her ringing Mum. It'd be better than a doorway or a bench.

Stella didn't look surprised when I said yes. 'All right, I'll show you tonight.'

Dot said, 'That's a turn up for the books, something doesn't smell right. Don't trust anything about that conniving little cow. I want to know it all tomorrow.'

16

The hall had a thick flowery-green and cream carpet. Under an oval mirror on the wall, there was little half-moon table with a cream telephone on it; behind the front door; a small toilet with a sink, next to that a kitchen, with a table and four chairs. Straight ahead was the living room, with a big window that faced onto the garden. On the wall above the telly, a shelf held a photograph of a man sitting at a table full of ale. Beside him, a blonde-haired woman wearing a black fur coat. Their glasses were raised, half-empty towards the camera.

Stella sat on a chunky gold, brocade chair. Two people could fit on it easily. Under the window I could see a long wooden cabinet on four stick legs. Everything was almost brand new. Stella watched me staring, lifted the lid up showed me inside. There was a turntable, and slots filled with LPs. If you took everything out, you could have lived in there. Lay down in it, legs dangling over the side.

I picked up some of the LPs. Johnny Cash, Elvis, Hank Williams; John Lennon. Slotted in one of the corners I saw a large bottle of whisky. 'Norm loves his music,' Stella said.

'Is he your dad?'

'Norm, nah, he's Mum's fella, was Mum's fella.'

'How many people live here?'

'Me and Norm.'

'Where's your mum?'

'Pissed off with Siggy.'

'Siggy?'

'He was Norm's best mate until he pissed off with that dirty little slag. C'mon, I'll show you how to work the washing machine. Then I'll show you your room. I sleep in it sometimes, if it gets noisy in the front room when the pub lets out.'

'Does Norm know I'm moving in?'

'I'll tell him when he gets home from work. He won't mind.'

'He might. Is this Norm's house? I don't think…'

'What? Just hold on and meet him. He won't mind. I know he won't.'

Stella ran into the hall once she heard Norm's key in the lock. She spoke in a low voice.

Norm padded into the living room in his grey stocking feet. With thick fingers he shook my hand, said he was pleased to meet me. He was the man in the photograph but his face now was fatter and he had less hair. His eyes were watery from the wind, he had a slanty smile. Norm sat on the settee, one leg up on the arm. Stella knelt, switched on the telly passed him the paper.

'Can't see the use in leaving that room empty,' Norm said, opening up the paper. 'Get your stuff and move in there tonight, the more the merrier, eh, Stella?'

'I can give five pounds a week,' I said.

Stella and Norm exchanged glances and smiled.

'Is that enough?' I said.

'More than enough,' Norm said. 'More than we had coming

in five minutes ago. It'll help keep the wolf from the door a bit longer, won't it Stella?'

Stella smiled her warmest smile at Norm.

Then he took the spare key out of his jeans pocket and handed it to me; like it was a worthless penny. 'Here you go; somebody might as well use it.'

After I'd said thanks, I made an excuse to leave the room. Sitting on the lid of the toilet, staring at the silver key in my palm, I blinked away the tears. Ten minutes ago I had nowhere to live. They didn't even know me properly. It was all a bit too much, this unexpected kindness.

Later that night, Stella told me that Norm got smashed on a Saturday. 'I mean legless, Robyn. I've had to leave him sometimes, all night on the living room floor, with a pillow and a blanket over him. He's a dead weight and I can't lift him. I wanted to warn you. It doesn't matter if I say take it easy tonight, Norm. He'll promise me he will, but when he comes home, it's a different story. It gets bad. I've just warned him, told him you'll scare Robyn.'

'That won't bother me, Stella, honest.' I said. And it wouldn't. What they didn't know was I'd seen plenty of bad stuff. Seeing Norm rotten drunk wasn't something that would frighten me.

'A couple of times, I've heard him crying. He starts calling that slag's name and it's… I mean you've seen this place, the way he is, bought her all this stuff. She chose it all. Half of it's still not paid for. He didn't know how to say no. We've had the phone disconnected, me and Norm trying to pay everything between us. And she's with that slimy bastard who came here for his tea, egg and chips, and free cups of Nescafe with two sugars if you please. Norm's best mate, he called himself. And all the while he was- I hate her guts.'

It went quiet for ages, and I understood why Stella was off with Dot, finally I said, 'When did she leave?'

'About seven weeks ago. Do me a favour; don't let them know in work. I can forget about things there.'

I thought about watching that funny film in the Odeon, and how good it felt to escape life for a little bit.

'I won't say a word.'

'Thanks.'

The bedding hadn't been washed because Stella's auburn number 9 hairs were in all different directions on the pillow. I turned it over and got between the sheets. My four carrier bags were behind the bedroom door. I hadn't unpacked yet, even though there was a narrow wooden wardrobe in the corner of the room. I wouldn't put my clothes in there. Norm still had time to change his mind, especially once he was drunk. Maybe he was a kick-off with ale. If the bags were by the door, I could be out of here in no time.

The one thing I was made up about was that I wasn't living on the streets. This thought made me feel better. There are other things you can do to make things better. Closing your eyes is a good thing to do. I closed mine, imagined living in Nan's; pictured myself lying on Nan's two-seater settee; tricked myself into believing I was home.

Some people in the centre of Liverpool lived in cardboard boxes. I'd seen them, early in the morning when I was on my way to work.

It's the cold that gets you, and the lack of sleep. You can manage being hungry, manage being scared. But once the cold gets inside your clothes, gets inside your bones, it feels like it's all over. You're scared to fall asleep then, in case the cold really gets you, and you don't wake up.

I opened my eyes, thought about how these musty pink sheets would be sloshing around tomorrow in the washing machine, and it made me smile.

Saturday morning I was in on my own. Stella worked in Waterford's until five. Norm worked eight until two in Bexlin's butchers on Robson Street. I got up as soon as I heard them leave for work at half-seven. Put Norm's records on low, sang, *Only the Lonely*. Got the hoover and the polish out, sang and danced along to the music. I did the downstairs first: toilet, kitchen, hall, finally, the livingroom. A real brick fireplace had been built along the front wall, a lecky fire slotted in the middle. Little lamps on round tables, Stella's mum had good taste in furniture. Cosy, was the word that I thought of.

I turned up the music, hoovered every room, opened every window; made all of the beds. Took Stella's pink bedding off, cleaned the bathroom, gathered up the dirty towels; threw a wash in the machine. I loved standing at the door of a room I'd just cleaned and looking; smelling polish in the air. It took me about an hour and a half to get the whole place spotless. I pulled the washing out of the machine, pegged it out on the line. By ten o'clock it was all done and I had the whole day to myself.

Central Station was already busy, I caught the train to Southport, was going to the second-hand shop to see if I could find a dress.

The lady who served me last time was polishing the glass counter. She smiled when she saw me. 'Looking for another dress?'

'Anything new in?'

'There are a couple of new ones you might like. Give me a minute.' She wore a plain black dress with a cream pearl necklace.

'I love that necklace,' I said.

'There's a string of pearls over there, in the cabinet. They're a little shorter than these.'

I saw them lying on lilac tissue paper. Nan always used to say pearls are for tears. 'Aren't pearls for tears?' I said.

She was searching a long rail of dresses, 'Supposed to be, if you buy them for yourself. You don't believe in all that do you?'

'Some of it.'

'How did you get on with the silk?'

'All right.'

'Good.' She handed me two dresses. 'Did you tell your friends where you got it?'

'No.'

'Didn't think so, you young ones. Try these. Let me see once you've got them on. I like the black boat neck.'

Both dresses were plain, a black one and an emerald green shiny one. I tried the green one on first.

'What fabric's this?' I asked. 'It's not silk.'

'No that's a lightweight satin. It's nice,' she said. 'Not sure about the colour on you and it will crease easily. Let me see the black.'

The black dress had a big swingy skirt that ended at my calf. My body took on a different shape, like it belonged to someone else.

'There, that's the one.' She said. 'You don't have to wear a new dress to become elegant. It's all about the cut. You suit kick-pleats. See here,' she pointed a few inches under my bra. 'This is where the bodice ends and the skirt begins, perfect for your shape. I know what I'm looking for now. When this cut comes in in a size ten, I'll keep them back for you.'

'Thanks, erm-'

'Claudia. And you are?'

'Robyn.'

'Well, Robyn, where are you going to wear this?'

'To a club in Liverpool: Gatsby's.'

'To meet a boy?'

I felt my face redden. 'He's eighteen.'

'Still a boy, dressed in big clothes.'

I laughed.

'You'll see,' she said. 'I know.'

I hurried back to the train station to go and see Rose, had to let her know where I lived. See if she'd come to Gatsby's with me tonight, hoped Alex would be there.

She smiled when I opened the door, put down the brush; linked her arm through mine. 'Everything all right, why didn't you come down last week, you seen Alex? I thought we were going to fabulicious?'

I called her into the back, explained where I was living and wrote down the address.

'Stella's all right but Norm, well, it's sly on him, he's so lovely Rose, but I'll tell you later. Come about half ten.'

Paula came into the back and put the kettle on. 'It's started to piss down out there. What're you two jangling about?' she said.

'Robyn's nan died,' Rose said.

'Ahh, did she, love?'

I nodded.

'What happened?'

'She went into hospital for an operation and-'

'Say no more. Hospital's too good a word for them places. Undertaker's friends I call them. Don't know how many of my customers I've lost through operations. It's costing me a fortune. I'd rather put up with the pain.' She went back into the salon, asked Rose to make her a cuppa once the kettle boiled.

'What're you wearing?'

'Dunno,' I said.

'Wanna see what our Rita had on last week, gorgeous. She copped off. If she doesn't wear it, I'll show you tonight.'

As I was leaving the shop, women sitting under hairdryers crinkled their noses up at me and said, 'Ahhh, poor thing.' Paula smiled at me through her mirror and waved. 'Come in early next week, I'll do you a wash and blow on the house.' The woman whose hair she was cutting waved, too. 'Or hold on a bit and I'll do it now.'

'Thanks, but I can't now,' I said.

'Why not, it won't take more than half an hour?'

'It's teeming. I have to get the washing in off the line.' In my hurry to get out, I tripped over a handbag and nearly fell. 'Thanks, bye,' I said and shut the door fast.

I didn't want sympathy or a free blow-dry. Things would never be the same now, without Nan. But everywhere else I wanted things to stay the way they were. That's probably why Stella wanted to keep what her mum had done away from Waterford's. There was nothing worse than the way they looked at you, their eyes making a bad noise, like you were cursed or something.

17

Rose knocked. I opened the front door, Norm falling in right behind her. Upstairs, I told Stella that he was in.

'Bevvied?' she said.

'Yeah,' I could hear the sloshing of bath water.

'He's one absolute pain in the arse. I'll be down now.'

In the livingroom, Norm was trying to untie his laces. The laces were treble knotted and as tight as you could tie them. He nearly fell over, but Rose gave me a hand to sit him down.

I untied his too-tight laces, slipped off his shoes; told Rose to get him a glass of water. Norm pointed at his turntable. I slipped an Elvis LP out of its sleeve. The first song was, *Suspicious Minds*. I lifted the needle up moved it onto: *Blue Suede Shoes*. Stella came in wearing pyjamas, a white towel wrapped around her hair. She rested both hands on her hips.

'All right, Norm?'

He didn't answer, was singing along to the music, nodding his head, index finger wagging in the air. '*Swonforthemoney, twoafortheshew, threetagetareadynwwww…*

That's what I loved about Norm, his passion for music. His

face had a huge smile on it while he sang; it did exactly the same for me.

I introduced Stella to Rose. 'Can you two hang on, only for a bit. Help me get the lord of the manor up to bed?'

Rose looked at me. 'Thing is we're meeting-'

'That's no problem,' I said. 'Is it, Rose? Long as we get the last bus in, we're okay.'

'Thanks, girls,' Stella said. 'Wanna drink?'

'Got any vodka?' Rose said.

We sat at the kitchen table and told Stella about Harry and Alex.

'Is that the lad who comes in the shop?' Stella said.

'Yeah, the one with the tie, looks like Bryan Ferry?' I said.

'He's gorgeous,' Rose said. 'But Harry's nicer. They took us for a meal in Chinatown.'

I laughed.

'What?' Stella said.

'Rose tried to eat this flannel thing with steam coming off it.'

Stella said, 'A what?'

Rose burst out laughing, 'I thought it was a pancake but it was for washing your hands.'

We all laughed.

'Felt like a right divvy. We didn't get in until about four in the morning.'

'Where're you staying tonight?' Stella said.

'Dunno. I've told my mum I'll be in Robyn's. She doesn't know I go to Gatsby's. Neither does my sister.'

'I don't mind if you stay here,' Stella said. 'But say goodnight to the lads before you come in, okay?'

'Okay, thanks,' Rose said.

'No worries.'

Twenty minutes later Norm was in bed still dressed. It took three of us to guide him up the stairs. Stella took his jacket off and draped it over a chair. He looked so small without it, fell fast asleep, the collar of his shirt upturned. What was it Claudia said, a little boy in big clothes? Finally, we made our escape to the bus stop.

This time the two bouncers at Gatsby's weren't having any of it. One of them laughed. 'Got your dinner money, and your school uniform in your bag, girls?' We could hear the music playing. Two girls walked past us and got in.

'We look older than them,' Rose shouted. 'They're only about ten. How come you let them in and not us?' The two bouncers loved it; Rose was giving them something to do, something to laugh at. One of them cupped his crotch and said dirty things and I wanted to leave. 'Let's go,' I linked my arm through hers. 'Are those clothes your Rita's?'

'No why?'

'Wanna try Cindy's?'

'Doesn't matter if I've got her gear on or not, she'll batter me anyway, for being in the same room as her.'

'What shall we do then?'

'Get a taxi back and finish Stella's vodka?'

'Okay. Or-'

'Or what?'

'If Cindy's is as big as Gatsby's, we could find a quiet corner on the dance floor away from your Rita.'

'Nah, she'll see me, or one of her mates will. We can't go there.'

'To be honest, Rose, I don't wanna go yet, been working all week. We've got ready, come into town, have money for a drink. C'mon, please, I wanna dance, have a good time.'

'Oh, all right. But if she's in there...'

'Do you realise I've just changed your mind for a lousy single vodka? You could have at least held out for a double. You're so cheap, Rose Mooney, nothing but a cheap night out.'

'Am I, now? We'll see about that once we get inside. I'm gonna order one of everything off the top shelf!'

Cindy's wasn't far from Gatsby's. The queue stretched right around the corner. From across the road we checked the queue for Rita and her mates, but there was no sign of her. At the door, a woman older than my mum sat behind a little desk. The one bouncer didn't give us a second look. We followed people in front of us down a flight of stairs. I looked back at Rose and smiled. 'That was easy.'

It was well smaller than Gatsby's. About thirty people on the dance floor and it was full. We didn't get near the bar before Rita and her mates pounced on Rose.

'Hey, you, shitty arse, what're you doing in here?'

Rose said, 'Same as you.'

Rita said, 'Out, now!'

Rose said, 'Make me.'

Rita said, 'Don't tempt me you little...'

Rose said, 'Tempt you what?'

Rita said, 'Cheeky bitch. I swear to God...'

Rita's mate laughed.

Rita said, 'Heard this one?'

Rita's mate said, 'Leave her.'

Rita said, 'What? She's a brassy little bitch.'

Rita's mate said, 'Leave her. We were in here at her age.'

Rose said nothing.

Rita looked at Rose. 'Go on then, piss off. Stay out of my sight. And if anyone asks, I'm not your sister.'

Rose walked towards the bar and I followed.

'Yessss!!!' I said.

Rose laughed. 'Double vodka and orange, love. She's paying.'

Even though we didn't get to see Harry and Alex we enjoyed ourselves. We had two drinks each, and danced all night until the DJ played the last song, which was a slowy. Rita didn't come near us and we stayed away from her. Just as we were leaving I looked back and saw Rita by the toilets, back pressed against the wall, kissing some lad.

Next morning, the sun peeping through the curtains woke me. I woke Rose up and we went downstairs; Norm was standing at the oven cooking bacon. His face was all blotchy and he hadn't changed his clothes.

'All right,' he said to me and Rose. 'Hungry?' Rose ran into the toilet by the front door, palm cupping her mouth. Norm smiled, 'Hangover?'

'She likes vodka, doubles.'

'Aw, paint stripper that stuff. Want some bacon?'

'She only had a couple. Any toast?'

Norm had two slices on a plate already buttered.

Rose came out of the toilet. 'I'm going, love. See yer.'

'Want me to walk you to the bus stop?'

'I'm all right.' She stood at the kitchen door. 'Thanks,' she said to Norm.

Norm looked at Rose's pale face. 'Wanna stay away from paint stripper.'

'Robyn, call in the shop?'

I didn't feel like going the shop, not for a little while anyway; until they forgot.

'You come here, Saturday night; half ten?'

'Okay. See you Saturday.'

The day passed quietly. I was upstairs for most of it, lying on top of the bed. Downstairs, Norm had the telly on low. I went down a couple of times to get a glass of water, could hear him snoring; smell the roast dinner cooking in the oven. I lifted the lids off two pans: carrot and turnip in one, mushy peas in the other. They were cooked and the electric ring was turned off.

Inside the oven, a roast chicken, skin too light yet, and a dish full of pale potatoes. When I saw that somebody had set the kitchen table for three, I went back upstairs, took my clothes out of the carrier bags, got the iron out of the kitchen, ironed them all then hung them up in the wardrobe.

I still needed to figure out how things worked here, had to remember this was somebody else's home. Norm could get annoyed and I could still be asked to leave. The best thing to do was make myself useful.

Stella was at the door. 'How did it go last night?'

'It ended up being a good night.'

'Didn't hear you come in. Did Rose stay?'

'Yeah, we were quiet.'

'Treat this place like it's your own you know, hiding in the bedroom all day.'

'Thanks.'

She sat on the bed. 'I do know how you feel, though. I felt like that when I came home from work and she'd gone. Norm was devastated. She's my mum and she did that. I thought he was gonna tell me to leave. I tiptoed around the place for a week, waiting for him to take it out on me. He didn't, he's not like that. In the end I said to him, don't you mind me being here, Norm? And he said no, love, anything's better than feeling lonely.'

'Ahh, did he? Nan used to say that when I lived there, said she liked the company.'

'Before she did that, I'd started saving for a place of my own. She's done it before, on my dad. A bigger wallet came along and she was out the door.'

'Was it Norm?'

'No. She had a couple more before Norm. I haven't met them all, but out of the ones I have met, Norm's the sweetest. He's even nicer than my dad. Anyway, I've got quite a bit saved up, a few hundred, and in a couple of years I'll have enough to buy furniture and pay rent on a place in advance. I fancy London.'

'You been there before?'

'Nah, but it looks exciting on the telly. That's why I want to become a manageress at Waterford's, not only can I save more because I'll get a rise, but there'll be a decent reference. Once I've had management experience, I can apply for good jobs in London. Reckon Maud has about six months left in her, maybe, before she retires.'

'Don't you have a fella?'

'I used to go with a lad but we argued, mostly over money he spent on nights out. I stay in most weekends and save my money. Once you've got your own place, nobody can tell you to leave.'

She curled the end of her fringe behind her ear, 'I'll get a fella in London when I'm ready. I'm only twenty. Everybody thinks that's old. But I'd rather be able to sort myself out, than sponge off men, like Dot, and that slag who calls herself my mother. Siggy had a massive win on the horses, like a few hundred. So off she skipped, slag. I swear, if it all goes tits up with Siggy and she tries to get back in here, I'll do time for that bitch!'

Stella went back to her room. She had the top twenty playing on the radio. Downstairs, I asked Norm if he wanted a cuppa.

He was watching a film, said he'd like that. When I came back in the livingroom I handed Norm his tea, sat down on a chair. He looked over at me, leaned forward; turned the telly down. 'Your room okay?' he said.

'It is. You don't mind me staying here, Norm?'

'Stay as long as you like.'

'Thanks.'

'Sorry, about your nan.'

'Yeah, thanks.'

I picked up my cup to cover my face but he caught me crying.

'I'm sorry, Norm.'

'Don't be. There's nothing wrong with having a good cry. Makes you feel better, I think.'

'I don't find that. I'm crying more now I realise I'm never seeing her again.'

'Takes a while to sink in, it's only been a couple of weeks for you.'

'But crying, like this–'

'You mean in front of me?'

'Yeah, I don't like to. Not just you, in front of people.'

'That's all right. I cried all the time when I lost my mam. Where's your mam?'

'In Edinburgh, she lives there with her fella, Owen.'

'You got no family here?'

'No. My mum was an only child.'

'And she left you?'

'She wanted me to go to Edinburgh, work in the pub. I was better off with May.'

'You didn't fancy Edinburgh?'

'I told her I was moving in with Rose once Nan died.'

'I see.'

'But they've got no room.'

'And your dad?'

I didn't answer. There were things I didn't know about my father, like where he was living. He was an invisible wave, so far out of sight he could've been mistaken for foam. The business of not having him around, and how he never behaved as he should grew thick in my mind. But I wanted to find him, didn't know where to begin.

'You don't have to tell me, I mean- stay here as long as you like. Rose is welcome to knock any time, all right?'

'That's great, I appreciate it.'

'It's tough without family, I know that. It's good to have somebody there, someone to turn to.'

'You have kids?'

'My wife, not Jean, Stella's mum, couldn't have kids. She died five years ago, on Christmas Eve. She was a girl, always a little girl. Dancing, singing; lit up a place from the minute she walked in. Drunken driver he was. Went for a drink after work and got behind the wheel. Too many times I've lost it on Christmas Eve. Fine one minute, then it just hits me, all of a sudden I'm bawling like a baby. And I'm a man. Men aren't supposed to cry.'

'I'm so sorry about your wife. What was her name?'

'Eileen, Eileen Anderson. We met when we were sixteen.'

'Sounds like she made you happy, Norm.'

'Nah, what made me happy was seeing her happy.'

He picked up his cup, held it to his mouth, his hand shook. 'So it's all right to cry,' he said. 'Nothing wrong with that because half the time life isn't fair, not one bit. And if you're dealt a duff hand, it's all right to cry, sometimes.'

When he'd finished, I took his cup into the kitchen and thought, there ought to be a Norm in every home.

Upstairs, I opened the bedroom window, looked into other people's gardens. Their own little bit of land. I imagined myself here in a season that was not winter. Spring, maybe, sitting out in the garden on a chair with a book, watching my bedding flap on the line, music on low, talking with neighbours over the wooden fences. Then I heard the words in my head. They said, *don't. Don't let yourself fall in love with this place.*

The smell of roast potatoes filled up the house. Nan would be made up I was here, and not on the streets. I couldn't help it, 'I love it here,' I said out loud.

My words made steamed up circles on the glass.

18

Monday, on my dinner, Dot wanted to know everything. 'What's her story? I mean, she keeps everything close to that scrawny little chest of hers. I know nothing about her.'

She asked me twenty questions about Stella. About boyfriends, her family, what the house was like, where about it was, until, in the end I said, 'Go and ask her yourself if you wanna know that much.'

Dot changed the subject once she saw I was in a mood. She went on about the weekend then, and Alex. 'We didn't go to Gatsby's so I didn't see him.' I tried to change the subject but she carried on.

'How can you expect to pay for nights out on your wage? You need a fella. Alex'll do for starters, to learn from. And maybe he'll be your base. But in the end, it's best to find somebody with money, as a backup. Money doesn't just talk, it gives orders. Now, let me show you eyeshadow.'

I let her put makeup on me but my heart wasn't in it. Alex probably copped off at the weekend, anyway. It didn't bother me if I never went to Gatsby's again.

Late in the afternoon, Alex came in. Stella went to serve him then looked at me, said she needed the toilet. I walked over and said, 'Yes, please?'

'Cheese pasty and a can of coke, please. Didn't see you Saturday?'

'No we went to Cindy's, you?'

'Gatsby's.'

I handed him the pasty, and the coke, 'Any good?'

'All right; we were looking for you.'

'Oh, we fancied a change, Cindy's was packed.'

'Never been there, might give it a try this Saturday, you going?'

'I might.'

Once he'd gone I turned to Dot. 'Show me eyeshadow again?'

Saturday, when I walked into the shop, some fella was giving Claudia a hard time, over a tape he'd bought that got all tangled up in his recorder. He wanted his money back, blamed the tape for ruining the recorder in his car. She took money out of the till. The man stood there with his palm held high, nearly up to Claudia's nostrils.

'Hello, Robyn,' she said. 'I've got something for you.'

The man lifted his palm higher, 'Any time today will do.'

Claudia said, 'I'm so sorry you were inconvenienced, you must have been looking forward to listening to the tape. I can only apologise.'

'Well,' the man said. 'I was.' He was a little calmer. 'It doesn't matter.'

After he'd gone I smiled at her. 'You didn't get a nark on with him? I would've started slamming things.'

'Kill them with kindness, that's what my mother told me.'

'It worked.'

'Yes, but I didn't do that years ago. Life could've been so much easier.'

'What do you mean?'

'My husband, the moaner, I call him. He screams that he doesn't like music on in the house, it gives him headaches, and the smell of paint makes him dizzy.' She opened up a small bag, placed a few brooches into the glass cabinet that was also the counter. 'He likes an untidy bedroom because climbing over his clothes in the morning means he gets some exercise. He complains about damp benches in the park he says cause piles. He thinks work colleagues are plotting to get him sacked, and he accuses me of trying to kill him.'

'With kindness?'

She laughed, and tiny crinkles formed on the outside of her eyes, 'With nagging.'

She went into the back and returned with a silver glossy dress. 'It's silk and it's going to be gorgeous on you. The lady who owns Biel's Jewellers passed a suitcase full of clothes in; they were her late mother's. This one has a Dior label, look, it's a nineteen-fifties number, try it on.'

'Dior?'

'French designer, very talented, had a heart attack eating his dinner, choked on a fishbone.'

'That's horrible.'

'Not really. It could've been worse. Fishbone sounds so elegant. Don't you think?'

Claudia was talking about death without making it sound scary.

I went into the changing room. The front of the dress had

a draped neck with a sparkly brooch at the centre. It was knee-length and swingy. The silver fabric changed with the light, sometimes becoming a pale iced blue. The neckline at the back swept low.

'Let me see? It's good, a good fit, a little big at the back. You have a shallow back. It needs a couple of one inch darts, here and here.'

'Won't it do? I'd like it for tonight.'

'It won't do. I'll put the darts in myself. You can't wear it hanging away from your body like that. It's worn like a second skin, silk. Let me pin it first.'

'There's no price on it.'

'It'll cost one pound, a bargain for a fully-lined Dior dress,' she winked.

When I came back out of the changing room, Claudia threaded a needle with silver cotton. I watched her sew the tiniest stitches down into a pointed triangle. Finished, she went over her first lot of stitches again. Somebody shouted for help, Claudia handed the dress to me. 'Here, you try with the second dart. Take your time. Just follow the pins.'

I sat down on a little stool at the side of the counter, followed the pins, making slightly bigger stitches than Claudia's. When it was finished, I put the dress back on and it was much snugger. 'Where did you learn how to sew?'

'My mother taught me when I was nine. I used an unthreaded machine first; made patterns with the needle hammering away through card. It got me used to using the foot and keeping the fabric on track. I don't sew much now, my eyes can't work as well as they used to.'

Claudia was so different from anybody I knew. I didn't go there because she got me dresses, I loved her way of thinking about things. She talked to me like I mattered, seemed interested in me and always had a smile. I liked that she'd had a different life to mine. Hearing about her husband, and Dior, and how she learned to sew was what I missed about Nan; her stories.

I paid Claudia the pound and said goodbye.

'I hope that boy appreciates the trouble you go to,' she laughed. 'You must stand out by miles in a sea of baggy jumpers and leg-warmers. That film, *Fame,* has got so much to answer for.'

Saturday night, I sat at the kitchen table waiting for Rose. It had gone eleven. She won't knock now, I thought, so I drank a vodka and orange with Stella. Norm came in drunk and we marched him straight up to bed. Stella took off his jacket and shoes, rolled him into bed and covered him. He was snoring before we closed his bedroom door.

Stella looked at my Dior dress and smiled. 'You've certainly got a look that's all your own,' she said.

I felt restless and wide awake.

Once Stella went to bed, I grabbed my key, opened the front door and headed into town. The last bus had gone. I caught a taxi down to Cindy's, had been looking forward to going out all week and having a dance. There would be no harm in it.

Cindy's was packed. I spied Alex and Harry at the bar.

'All right, Robyn,' Harry said. 'Where's Rose?'

'Dunno, I waited but she didn't show up.'

'Oh, who are you with?'

I didn't know what to say, hadn't thought this through properly, couldn't even get up and dance, not on my own. It sounded desperate, now, saying I was on my own.

'My mate, Stella, she's gone the toilet.'

Alex turned around holding two pints. 'All right, wanna drink?'

'I'm okay. I'll get one in a minute.'

'Where's Rose?'

'I just told Harry, she was meant to knock at mine.'

Harry waved across the room at a lad. 'Be back now,' he said to Alex, taking his drink.

After a while, Alex looked across at the toilets, fixed his eyes on me, 'You on your own?'

'Behave. My mate's in the toilet, didn't you hear me?'

'You're on your own, aren't you?'

'No.'

'You are.'

'Yes.'

He frowned.

'What?'

'That's not normal.'

'Normal?'

'For a girl, I mean.'

'Why? I like it here, the music, dancing. What's bad about that? I'd say it's normal to wanna go out and have fun after you've been working all week.'

'But you're a girl, on your own in a nightclub. Everyone knows girls don't just walk into a club on their own. Surely your mum's told you that? I'm sure she never went on her own when she was your-'

'I'm not my mum!' My voice sounded harsher than I'd meant.

'All right! You don't have a clue, do you?' He pushed his hand inside his pocket, offered me a pound note.

'I can buy my own drink.'

'I didn't mean–'

I looked away from him.

'Nice dress.'

I said nothing.

'You're not speaking to me now?'

'Who makes these rules?'

'What?'

'Telling people they can't come out, women they can't come to a club on their own? So if my mate doesn't turn up, and I haven't got a fella, and I'm all ready to go out, I have to stay in because I'm female? We're not Victorians, Alex; it's nineteen-eighty for Christ's sake.'

'Dickheads everywhere once this club lets out, drunken dickheads.'

'Well that's their problem isn't it, not mine.'

I turned away, thought of the man who tried to attack me, what Alex had said made some sense, but I'd never tell him that. What happened to all the women who ended up with nobody? Did they sit in front of a telly all their lives? What places could they go on their own?

The DJ was playing Blondie, *The Tide Is High*, and I wanted to dance. I bought a vodka, drank it in two goes; left the glass on the bar. When I turned back around Alex had gone. Coming here wasn't such a great idea after all. One of Rita's mates walked past with another girl. 'You with Rose?' she asked me.

'No, she isn't here. Is Rita here?'

'No. Who're you with then?'

I thought about asking to dance with them but changed my mind when I saw how they were looking at me. 'No one,' I said.

'You've walked in here on your own like some divvy little slag?'

'What's it to you?'

Both girls glared at me then Rita's mate said, 'Wearing her nan's dress an' all: scrub-a-dub-dub.' They walked away, across to a gang of girls standing by the DJ. They pointed at me and I wondered why everything was such a big deal. Opening my bag, checking my key and my money, I walked to the stairway that led up to the street.

Outside, people were still queuing to get in. It wasn't raining, so I decided to walk home and save my money. Somebody was calling my name, turning, I saw Alex.

'Thanks for letting me know you were going.'

'I need permission to leave as well?'

'You're a narky cow.'

'Am I, wonder why?'

'Where're you going?'

'Nowhere.'

'Look, I'm sorry.'

'What for?'

'I should've at least said I'm made up to see you.'

'Are you?'

'Yeah, made up you're out. Come on. Let's walk through here.'

He took hold of my hand; I pulled it away, folded my arms in front of me. He walked up the steps and into the gardens.

'I'm not going in there,' I said.

'Why? C'mon, I won't bite.'

The thought of what that man tried to do to me made me shudder. 'I said no.'

He linked his arm through mine in a playful way, 'All right, let's go up to the Walker then.'

A trail of lamp posts lit the way. We sat down on a cold bench by the Walker Gallery. I held my breath, angry, and scared at the same time, felt my heart rocking, tried to calm down. I was glad when Alex spoke. 'That place used to be a cemetery years ago,' he said, 'my dad told me. He's a gravedigger.'

Whenever anybody spoke about their dad, it made me feel sad. I dreamed of meeting my dad one day, to be able to fill up a room with the real him; and not just the man I had to imagine.

'They left some of the dead and built the gardens over them.'

I thought about how I might have been killed in there.

'Why did they do that?'

'It got too full. You know something?'

'What?'

'I go to graveyards, a lot.'

'Why?'

'I like reading the gravestones, they fascinate me.' He looked into my eyes, 'You think that's creepy?'

'Not creepy, different.'

'Most people do. Morbid, my mum used to say, you have a fascination that's not normal for a young lad.'

'There's that word, normal, again. Why does everything have to be normal? What is normal anyway?'

'Normal's doing what everyone else does.' He leaned in close to me. I could smell shampoo and beer. 'Nothing wrong with normal,' he kissed my hair. His lips moved down my face and I thought: he's taking off my tinted moisturiser. It took me ages to get it right, it'll go all patchy. He kissed one corner of my lips, then the other. Then he kissed me full on the lips. Then I didn't care about my tinted moisturiser. His mouth was warm and soft and I kissed him back. I heard voices, pulled away from him. A gang of girls and lads walked past, heading to Cindy's. They didn't see us.

Shuffling away from him, I said, 'I need to go.' But I didn't stand up.

'Not yet.'

'I have to.'

He shimmied along the bench next to me. 'Everything all right, why've you been off work?'

'My nan died.'

'Oh, erm, sorry to hear that.'

'It's all right.'

Two police cars rushed by, blue lights flashing; after a while it got cold, my nose felt it first.

'Listen,' he said, 'a wood pigeon.'

It was such a strong cooing sound I felt it touch my chest. Alex moved closer and put his arm around me.

'You've left Harry back there,' I said, nodding towards Cindy's.

'He's okay. He's with his cousin. Want me to walk you home?'

'It's miles out of your way. I'll get a taxi.'

'At least let me walk you to London Road. You'll get one up there.'

Once we got to London Road, we stopped outside Selway's bingo. A couple of taxis raced by but I didn't put my hand out. We stepped into the doorway of the bingo and kissed again.

'I've got to go, now, sorry,' I said, flagging a cab.

He opened the taxi door and I sat down on the back seat.

'So, you busy walking through graveyards tomorrow, Alex?'

'All afternoon.'

'You wanna know something?' I said.

'What?'

Alex had hold of the door, body stooped, head inside the cab. 'I wear dead people's clothes.'

'Yeah?' he laughed. 'I'm sure they don't mind.'

And we both laughed. When the cab pulled away I waved to him out of the back window; watched his face rushing away from me, thought about how I should've stayed a bit longer. There would always be next time, though. I was glad I'd gone out, was grinning like a lunatic and didn't care.

The taxi driver stared at me through his mirror. 'My wife wouldn't be caught dead in somebody else's clothes,' he said. I carried on grinning. Then he said, 'Neither would I. Pair of crackpots.' He didn't speak another word.

Nobody was up when I got in. I hung up the silk dress, washed off what was left of my tinted moisturiser, fell asleep feeling the happiest I'd felt in a long time. Couldn't help wondering what had happened to Rose.

19

Sunday afternoon. Rita opened the door eating a bowl of soggy Weetabix; she pointed the spoon at me. 'What do you want?'

'Is Rose in?'

She shouted down the hall. Rose came to the door in her pyjamas, eyes all red and blotchy. Rita punched me with her eyes, walked back inside.

'You okay?'

'No.'

'What's the matter?'

She took in a big breath; stared at me but said nothing.

'Get dressed. I'll wait for you. We can take a walk.'

Rose said okay.

I sat down on the step. Rita stood behind me. 'Nice mate you are.'

'What?'

'Don't what me. Supposed to be her mate, look after each other. Where were you, eh?'

'You mean last night?'

'I mean when that piece of shit let his dick out without its coat on.'

Rose stood behind Rita, a jacket over her pyjamas. She pushed past her.

'Shut your big gob. It's not Robyn's fault.'

We walked down the street; heard Rita slamming the front door and kicking it over and over again. I didn't speak until we were far enough away. 'What's not my fault?'

'Nothing.'

'Rose, what's the matter?'

'Just can't believe it, my first time. I'm having a baby.'

I stopped walking. 'With Harry?'

'With Simmo, that time in the park, remember?'

'Yeah, but you said you went home not long after-'

'I lied.'

'You sure you're pregnant?'

'I've had the test.' Rose's eyes filled with tears. She started to cry. I'd never seen Rose cry. I linked my arm through her arm.

'Oh, Rose, It'll be okay.'

'I'm not even seventeen. It's like some sort of sick joke.'

She seemed, and looked, eighteen. Shoulders up to her ears, hands pushed deep inside her pockets, head bent low, today she could have been mistaken for twenty.

'Does Simmo know?' I asked.

'No. And I don't want him to know. He's with Dawn McLoughlin now. Thinks he's God's gift. I love Harry, can't stop thinking about him. And I don't know if he likes me or not, properly, I mean.' Rose looked down at her belly.

'And now: this.'

We walked for a bit not saying a word, stopped outside a shop.

'Want something?'

'Nah, you?'

'Not hungry. Have you seen Harry?'

I was going to tell Rose that I went to Cindy's without her last night, but changed my mind. Tried to think of something to do that would cheer her up.

We both said nothing for a long time. Finally, it was Rose who broke the silence. 'I feel sick. You mind if I go back home? I'm tired.'

'Okay. I'll take you to Cindy's Saturday? We'll have a laugh, eh?'

Rose pulled her arm out of mine and walked away down the street. 'Don't say that. Once you say that out loud it doesn't happen.' She was crying again, carried on walking away. 'Remember what happened to Caroline? Everyone will know soon.'

'Sorry, Rose.'

She shouted back at me. 'What're you sorry for? It was my own stupid fault. I could kick myself up and down this bastard street.'

We knew a girl, Caroline, her name was. She'd dropped out of our school to have her baby at fourteen. Everyone said she was a slag because she'd done it with a nineteen year-old man at her sister's birthday party. Then the talk was she'd had six boyfriends and didn't know who the father was. After she left school, the stories faded. I'd seen her in town pushing a pram. She looked so young. Her little girl must have been two now. But she had no mates and no fella, went everywhere with her mum.

I watched as she hurried away, hoped that wouldn't happen to Rose, she was my best friend.

20

Norm liked company. So I needn't have worried about getting in his way. When he was watching telly, and me and Stella were talking in the kitchen he'd shout, 'Stella, Robyn, come and see this.' It was usually a shootout, or a funny scene from one of the old cowboy films. He loved John Wayne. Made his hand into a gun, pointed it at the screen, shot the bad guys and laughed. He watched Clint Eastwood films, and sometimes he said the lines along with Clint. When the next programme came on, if it didn't interest him, he'd say, 'What a load of punks.'

After the films finished, he'd put his records on, me and Stella sang along with him, mostly to Roy Orbison, Elvis, or John Lennon. Then he'd open his whisky, and have a little swig.

Norm was a brilliant cook. He brought cut-price meat home from Bexlin's butchers most days. With the ham shanks, he would make pea and ham soup. He made corned beef hash, curried scouse and shepherd's pie. My favourite was his roast chicken dinner on a Sunday. The potatoes were crispy on the outside and fluffy on the inside. He made apple crumble and custard on a Sunday, sometimes. We sat in front of the telly with him, watched old Laurel and Hardy and Cagney films. He had this laugh, a bit like a clap to begin with then it ran away into a machine gun. It was a laugh you had to join in with.

One Saturday I saw him, face in his palms, weeping and saying why, over and over. I sat down next to him.

'Are you all right, Norm?' I said. 'Can I get you anything?' He stopped crying but he didn't answer, didn't take his palms away from his face, so I left the room. Stella said he avoided thinking about stuff all week, and once Saturday came, the shit hit the fan.

'The problem is,' she said, 'he thinks he's dealing with it but he's not, better that he loses it here, than in a pub. I'm never getting that attached to anyone, ever, not if it does that to you. She hasn't even said sorry, selfish cow.'

In work, when Stella and Maud went out, I told Dot about Rose having a baby.

'She still with the fella?'

'No.'

'It's all over for her, then. Gone and ruined her life for a cheap thrill.'

Alex walked in. Dot watched me serve him, 'Yes, please?'

'You get home all right Saturday?'

'Yeah, you?'

'Went back to Cindy's for an hour.'

'Oh.'

'It was boring.'

'Can I get you anything?'

'Just came in to see you.'

'Well, you've seen her,' Dot said. 'You're holding up the queue.'

Alex turned around, there was nobody behind him. He gave Dot a funny look, 'See you Saturday, Robyn.' he said.

Once he left Dot started cleaning the glass doors on the oven, 'You make sure you get yourself to the doctor and ask for the pill.'

'I'm not doing anything.'

'Doesn't matter, best to be safe than sorry, I'll come with you. I'll say I'm your mum and I want you on the pill.'

'I'm fine.'

'Don't schools teach young girls anything? Get to the doctor and ask for the pill. It can happen as fast as that,' she clicked her fingers on 'that'. 'I'm telling you. Get you drunk so you don't know what you're doing. Get the pill or you'll end up preggy same as your mate.'

I couldn't get pregnant, ever, having no home. But she was right. Rose was drunk in the park and she didn't listen to me. I wouldn't get pregnant, and wasn't taking any pills. Kissing was all I wanted and you couldn't get preggy from kissing. Dot thought otherwise.

'It's what comes after kissing you've got to worry about. One thing leads to another. Wear drawers with tight elastic in the legs. Wear two pairs. And don't get pissed, that's when the fun really begins. And it'll be you left holding the baby.'

There were plenty of things about Dot that made me feel uncomfortable, especially what she was doing with Ron Fairbrother. But she had a point. I was going to do everything I could to avoid getting pregnant, no matter what.

Saturday morning, I was on the Southport train going to see Claudia; had cleaned around everywhere and put the washing on the line.

I imagined Claudia had three dresses for me to choose from.

All silk. When I got to the shop, she wasn't there. A man stood inside the window wriggling an off-white wedding dress onto a mannequin. 'Is Claudia here?' I asked.

He peeped above the mannequin's shoulder. 'Sorry, she called in sick. Can I help?' He stepped down from the window.

'No, it's all right; she usually has dresses for me but…'

'Oh, are you Robyn?'

'Yes.'

'There is one, she's put it behind for you.'

He handed me a white plastic bag. 'Check in there.'

I took a dress out of the bag. It was a sky blue dress size ten.

'You can try it if you want.'

'It's all right. I'll take it, how much?'

'It's a pound.'

'Thanks. Is Claudia all right?'

'Not sure, she rang me early this morning asking me to cover for her.'

'Will you say I said thanks?'

'I will. She'll probably be back next week so you can tell her yourself.'

Sitting on a bench on the platform, I felt sad that I hadn't got to see Claudia, hoped she was all right. Inside my bones, I felt something wasn't right with her, but couldn't figure out why. I'd caught her a few times looking into the distance, letting go of a sigh that seemed to dissolve right back inside her body.

Rose was using a comb to scrape hair out of a load of brushes. She had dark circles under her eyes. 'You okay?'

'Don't mention anything to Paula, couldn't stand another lecture.'

'What's wrong?'

She put her lips right up to my ear and whispered, 'My mum wants me to have an abortion.'

'And you?'

She flopped down into a chair. 'I don't know. It's-' her eyes filled with water. 'I don't think I can…the more I think about it… our Rita's saying, have it then and give it up for adoption.'

Paula shouted Rose to fetch the brush for the floor.

'We can't talk here. Come to Norm's tonight, about ten?'

'All right, don't fancy Cindy's though.'

'Okay.' I said.

Rose knocked about ten o'clock. Norm was out and me and Stella were watching telly. I'd told Stella about Rose and she said she'd have a talk with her. Rose looked calmer, her skin was clear and smooth, like she'd had a good sleep. She took off her coat and sat next to me on the settee. Stella turned the telly off. 'You all right, Robyn's told me. What's your mum said?'

'She's telling me to have an abortion.'

'What other choices do you have?'

'Have the baby and keep it, or have the baby and give it away.'

'It's your decision.'

'I know. I can't choose and my sister wants me to give the baby away.'

'And you want…?

'I don't want that. My kid with somebody else, people I don't know. I'd always worry that the kid wasn't happy, or when it grew up it would come and find me, and hate me for giving them away.'

'So, it's keep the baby or an abortion?'

'What would you do?'

Stella didn't answer straight away. Rose looked at me and I said nothing.

'I don't know,' Stella said. 'Until it happens to you- see I think you know yourself, Rose. I'd know what to do if it happened to me.'

Rose looked at me again. 'Robyn?'

'I'm like you; I couldn't give a kid away. But I couldn't be a mum, not yet.'

'My mum said it's only as big as a fingernail. It's not a proper baby yet.'

'Do you think you can do it, be a parent?'

'I think I can. I think I can but-'

Stella's voice was soft. 'No butts, Rose. If you think you can be good for this kid then keep it. If you think you'll get narky because you had a kid too early, well-'

'I won't get narky. It's not the kid's fault.' She looked at me. 'It's not the kid's fault one bit. I want to keep it.' Then she was sobbing. I put my arms around her, 'You'll be all right.'

Stella went into the kitchen to make us a drink. I followed her, 'I don't know what I would've done without you, Stella. You're a good mate.'

'Don't be daft,' she said. 'It's nothing.'

We watched a film together and chatted, until Norm was singing on the front step. Stella stood up. 'Here we go, rock 'n' roll,' she said.

'Thanks, Stella,' Rose said. 'Thanks so much.'

'Feel better?'

'I do. I feel much better.'

'Good. Robyn, help me get happy Larry up the stairs will you?'

then she looked at Rose and smiled. 'You stay where you are, can't take any risks now, not with someone in your condition.'

One week later, Rose told me she'd had an abortion. Her mum threatened to kick her out if she didn't. And Rita was backing up everything her mum said, so she was left with no choice. The following Saturday, we went to Cindy's early. She got rotten drunk too quick on vodka and orange. When she knocked for me I could tell she'd already had a drink.

Before Alex or Harry came in, and before her Rita and her mates came in, I took Rose back to Norm's in a taxi, put her in my bed, and slept on the settee. In the early hours I heard her crying. I got into the bed, put my arms around her. 'It's all right. You cry all you want.'

She said sorry for spoiling my night, told me she couldn't sleep; said her baby was a little girl, a little girl who looked like her, not Simmo. She said she had pains in her belly where the baby once was. And she had bad thoughts about the baby waiting somewhere for her to come, because it was, after all, alive. 'They make me take the pill. Both of them standing over me in the kitchen like the pill police, making sure I swallow, checking under my tongue for Christ's sake. I'm never getting pregnant again, I swear.'

The thing was she'd made up her mind here, that night, with me and Stella, had made a choice, the right choice for her. And it was sad, how the big choices about what happened to your baby had nothing to do with you, even though it was your body, and you were the one who had to live with how it all turned out.

21

Her smile was heavy and put on like an extra job. I walked over and said hello to Claudia, handed her a box of Dairy Box. 'Thanks for keeping that sky blue dress behind for me. It's my favourite.'

'No, you shouldn't have, really. You can't afford these. Thanks, Robyn, but you really shouldn't-'

She took a hanky out of her bag, dabbed it around her eyes. 'You okay? It's only chocolates.'

'Yes, sorry, I had a lady come back in for a hat earlier on. She'd worn it on her wedding day and changed her mind about giving it away. I told her it wasn't in the window more than twenty minutes and it sold. She started crying. What could I do? You can't decide you don't want something one minute; then expect it to still be there the next.'

'I don't suppose she thought somebody else would've taken it that fast,' I said.

'No, I don't suppose she did.' She took out a green bag.

'Look, I've found a wonderful silk for you. It's a dusky pink colour but just look at that beading around the neckline. It's been sewn on by hand. It must have taken hours.'

Tiny cream and deep pink beads were sewn in eight rows around the neckline. 'That's lovely, so delicate.'

'The quality in the satin lining is incredible. You could make an evening dress from the lining alone.'

I tried it on, showed Claudia and she clapped her hands. 'I'll get that for you, as a thank you for the chocolates.'

'But they were a gift.'

'I want to. It would make me feel better.'

'Anyone serving here?' an elderly lady gave Claudia a dirty look, tapped her money on the glass counter. Claudia turned her head towards the counter and a bit of her neck scarf slipped down. I saw dark blue-black marks. She caught me looking, pushed the scarf back up and walked away.

I was inside the changing room for ages. She knew I'd seen the marks and I didn't know what to do. When I finally came out, Claudia was in the window.

'There's a bag on the counter for the dress. It's all paid for. Bye, Robyn, see you next week,' she shouted.

When I got to the train station, there was no train in, so I sat on a bench and waited.

Once the train arrived, people rushed to get on, I watched it pull out of the station, got up; made my way back down to Lord Street. When Claudia saw me at the door, she asked me to follow her into the back.

'Robyn, I'm sorry. I think you've got the wrong idea. You see my husband has, well, we have a cat, and sometimes he-'

'Cats scratch. They're not scratches, Claudia. Somebody's had hold of you by the neck; I just want to know if you're okay?'

'I'm fine.'

'You sure? I just-'

'What, you've just what? Come to save me? What do you know, you're just a girl?'

I know more than you think, I wanted to say, but felt cheeky. Mum had a man before Owen. When he had the ale in him, he got violent, hitting her became part of every Saturday night then he started hitting me. It wasn't easy, but eventually she got rid of him, once she realised he was never going to change.

'I can't save you. You have to do that yourself. Whatever he's told you, but I'm guessing now, maybe he's said sorry and it won't happen again? Not true. Maybe he's asked for another chance because this time he'll try harder? Not true. He'll do it again, Claudia. He will. Next time you might not be so lucky.'

The shop door opened, a customer walked in and Claudia rushed away from me.

'The whole thing's just so silly, now really, no more of this. I have to get back on the shop floor.'

22

It was December, and the rain hadn't stopped all morning. Maud said we should be grateful it was rain and not snow. I was three months into my government scheme, exactly half way. Dot had been the post office for change; her umbrella dripped tiny puddles all over the tiled floor. It had been quiet, hardly anyone out on the streets. Maud came and joined me and Dot on our break. She sat on a high wooden stool, sipping a cup of tea.

'Now your, dropping things all over the floor phase is over, I can honestly say you're one of the best young people we've had working here.'

I glanced at Dot and she smiled.

'I'm going to put in a good word with Mr Fairbrother, ask him not to finish you up in March. What do you say? Would you like to work here on a permanent basis?'

'Do you think there's a chance?'

'If you don't ask, you don't get. You can add up a large order in your head, and you're good with people. At the next meeting, I'll make sure he hears about how great you're doing. Who knows, you could own the business one day. Aim high, that's what I say.

Imagine; I've been a manageress for years. Two holidays a year: a beautiful house, my own car, a nice husband like my Harold. The harder you work, the better you play, and you don't owe anyone anything.' Then her voice sounded like a snatch. 'Isn't that right, Dot?'

Dot said nothing. When Maud went back onto the shop floor, Dot said, 'What the hell was that all about?'

I started laughing, 'I don't know.'

'I'm not joking. Can't wait until we close up, I'm bored stiff with this place. You, ending up with somebody like her Harold? Ha! Maud and Harold are living a life so brilliantly fucking dreary, they've buried themselves alive!'

Mr Fairbrother hadn't been coming in the shop as often as he used to. Stella said there'd been rumours he was with another shop assistant in the St Michael's Market shop, well younger than Dot. Stella heard that Dot asked Mr Fairbrother to leave his wife for her, but he refused. He'd gone cold on Dot now, Stella said, and was sorry he ever got involved with her.

Maud shouted Dot's name.

Dot checked her watch. 'What's her problem, now; we've got six minutes left.'

Stella stuck her head around the door, said in a sly voice, 'There's someone here to see you, Dot.'

On the other side of the counter, a short man wearing glasses held a little boy up against the glass counter to Dot, his anorak was saturated. 'We were passing and he wanted to see where his mum works.' The little boy had a ring doughnut in his hand, his face lit up when he saw Dot. 'Sorry, we're busy here, Malcolm, I can't stop.'

'He only wants a hug.'

'You take your time,' Stella said to Dot, 'I'll serve.'

Maud came out of the back wearing her coat. 'Won't be long, going the shop,' she said. 'We need teabags.'

'He's a handsome young fella. What's his name?' Stella asked.

Dot ignored her, leaned over the counter and kissed the little boy.

'Joseph,' Malcolm said.

Dot was edgy, shuffling cakes around. 'I need to get on, sorry; pick up some chops for our tea will you?'

Through the window I watched Mr Fairbrother parking his black Mercedes. Dot was fussing over Joseph's zip on his coat, didn't see him walking towards the door.

Stella looked out of the window and grinned.

When Dot saw Ron Fairbrother walking through the door, all colour disappeared from her face. He marched right past us and slammed the door shut.

Malcolm said, 'Who was that?'

'Nobody, Mal, better get him home. You know what he's like when he gets hungry.'

Malcolm looked at the doughnut in Joseph's hand, looked back at Dot, a confused expression on his face.

'Dot!' Mr Fairbrother shouted from the back.

Dot shut her eyes tight.

'Can you come out here, I need to see the books!'

She didn't move. Malcolm stared at her. Joseph mashed the cake into the side of Malcolm's face and laughed. Did it again, knocking his glasses sideways.

'You're being shouted there, Dot,' Stella's eyes had a dark sparkle. Then Stella looked right at Malcolm. 'If that passageway could talk it would scream,' she said.

He gave Dot a bad look.

The air was so thick it clogged up my throat. You needed a mask to breathe it in, bit by bit.

'I'll get the books for Mr Fairbrother, Dot,' I said.

Stella grabbed my arm, 'Stay where you are, Robyn. You know only Dot knows where the books are kept.'

Dot turned around, looked at Stella with astonished baby eyes. 'Thanks Robyn, love,' she said, reaching inside her overall pocket, handed Malcolm a crumpled tissue for his face. 'I'll have to get on, sorry.'

He didn't take the tissue.

Mr Fairbrother shouted Dot's name again. 'You coming, Dot, I don't have all day?'

Malcolm walked away, turned to cut Dot with his eyes, Joseph twisting and turning in his arms; screaming.

23

Saturday, I wanted to clean around and get the tree up, wasn't planning on visiting Claudia after giving her all that advice last week. I'd felt bad on the train ride home. Who was I to stand there and tell an adult what to do? You could see on her face she was upset. I'd wait a couple of weeks, then go back to make sure she was okay.

I unpacked the tree first, draped it with red tinsel and hung the baubles on, stood it next to the telly; put John Lennon on, hung the rest of the decorations, made a cup of tea and sat down. I was lucky to be living here.

Stella brought a chippy in for me and Norm. We ate it in front of the telly. 'It looks great in here,' Norm said.

Stella said, 'Brill isn't she, Norm?' She gave me a big smile.

Rose knocked about half past ten. One of the customers from Curl Up-n-Dye brought her new baby in to show Paula. She let all of the staff have a hold, Rose stayed hidden in the toilet, because nobody in work knew about her abortion. After the lady had left, Rose didn't fill up or anything, just got on with her work.

'I step off the bus to come here, and all of a sudden I can't stop crying,' she said. Stella gave her some tissues, poured her a drink.

'Why don't you get dressed up and come with us to Cindy's, Stella?' Rose said.

'I'm too old for Cindy's. It's full of little kids.'

'Our Rita goes. She's your age.'

Stella laughed. 'I've got better things to spend my money on, thanks.'

'Aw c'mon, just this once.' I said. 'It'll be a…'

'Don't,' Rose said.

'I'm quite happy here with my vodka and the telly. You two go and enjoy yourselves.'

Harry and Alex were standing by the bar when we got to Cindy's. Rose scanned the room. 'You see her?' she said to me. I spotted her on the dance floor with one of her mates. 'She's over there. Look.'

'Right, we'll stay this side of the room.'

Harry stood by the bar, a pint of beer in his hand. 'All right, girls, wanna drink?'

I took the money out of my bag. 'No thanks, I've got it.' Rose was talking to Harry.

Alex said, 'Long time, no see.'

'I know. We haven't been out.'

He looked at my dress; the dusky pink silk Claudia bought for me, 'Bet you've been dying to wear that.'

I laughed. 'Where've you two been?'

'Around, pubs, can't remember.'

He was drunker than usual, words gravelly and long. 'So, wanna dance?'

I ordered and paid for our drinks, handed Rose hers.

'Let me drink this, get up for the next one?'

We stayed on the dance floor for five songs straight. Alex was funny; waving his arms, messing about: stumbling a couple of times, but he didn't fall. Then he walked away from me, pretended to leave the dance floor, came back again, twirling my arm over my head, twirling himself and clapping to the beat. When we got back over to the bar, Rose had three empty vodka glasses by her. I looked at her eyes; all wobbly. Harry still had the same pint.

'You okay, Rose?'

She lifted her glass up in front of her face: 'Top of the pops.'

I looked across at her Rita, staring over.

'Need the toilet, Rose?'

'Nope!'

'Well I do. Come on.' Linking my arm through her arm, I ushered her into the toilets, slammed the lid down on the seat, sat Rose down; locked the door, stooped, voice low, taking her face in my hands. She was holding onto the glass tight. 'You've had enough vodka. Your Rita's here and she's watching.'

'Shite on our Rita,' she said. 'She can go and-'

'Remember the park? You've drank too much too fast and Harry's here. You need to think. You could end up preggy again for Christ's sake.'

She hiccupped. 'I'm on the pill.'

'So that's all right then is it, because you've taken the bloody pill?'

'You told me you wished you'd come back to my nan's that time with Simmo. Your Rita will pound you if you get preggy again, she'll batter you, Rose, and your mam'll kick you out, you listening?'

'Whose side are you on?'

She looked down at the floor, jiggled the ice about in her glass. Neither of us spoke, our words hung in the air. I couldn't give up, had one last go at changing her mind.

'For fuck's sake, Rose, this time won't you listen?'

She looked stunned. 'You're swearing?'

'I am fuckin' swearing.'

'But you never, I mean, oh God. What am I doing? What's wrong with me?' She stared down into her glass. 'I'll pour this down the sink and have an orange juice. Then we can dance.'

Somebody banged on our door. 'C'mon, hurry up in there, pregnant woman out here.'

Rose hugged me. 'I'm such a loser.'

'No, you're not. You made one mistake. You're allowed to make mistakes. But I won't let you make another one, not while you're with me. Stop looking at the floor, look at me. I left you last time, and I shouldn't have, I messed up. You're stronger than this, Rose; you're so much stronger than this. Don't go soft on me. Don't you dare give up and fall to the bottom of a fuckin' glass; you hear me?'

Rose nodded, tears fell down her face.

'Now, stand up, wipe your snotty nose, and let's get out of here. Just me and you. No more drinks.'

Rose dabbed her face with the back of her hand. 'Don't you wanna dance, you love dancing?'

I opened the cubicle door, walked over to the sink and tipped her drink away. She splashed water on her face and smiled at me through the mirror.

Harry and Alex were waiting outside the toilets for us.

'She okay?' Harry asked.

'Fine, just tired I think, been on her feet all day.'

'Take a walk?' Alex said.

I looked at Rose then across to where her Rita was, she wasn't looking in our direction. 'I'm going home, Alex. I'm shattered as well, sorry.'

They followed us outside onto the street. Alex put his arm around me. He reeked of ale. I hated the smell of it on him, hated seeing him this drunk. 'Ahh, don't go yet.' We walked towards St John's Gardens. 'Take a walk through here?' Alex said when we reached the gate. Harry stood next to Rose.

I saw a taxi turning the corner and stuck my hand out. Alex grabbed my hand and clamped it around his waist, pulled me into him too close, kissed me too hard on my lips and it hurt. He lifted me up, stumbled, pushed my back into the wall, tried to kiss me again. I pushed him off, took a step back, pushed him in the chest, the cab whizzed right past.

Harry was laughing.

I glared at Harry. 'What are you laughing at?'

Harry apologised.

'Come on, Rose, let's go.'

Walking towards London Road, I saw another taxi and put my hand out. It pulled over, Rose got in first, stumbled to the floor. I helped her onto the seat.

'She okay?' the driver asked.

'Yeah, she slipped.'

Through the back window I watched Alex and Harry swaying back towards Cindy's.

'Bye, Harry,' Rose shouted through the back window, 'my

lovely, lovely Harry.' She rested her head on my shoulder, closed her eyes. 'They'll probably get off with new girls, now.'

'Good! Alex is a right divvy when he's drunk.'

'So am I, next week I'll just drink coke with nothing else, promise. Naked coke, ha.'

'Think Christmas Eve will be the next night out for me; we could have a meal before.'

In school Rose was always the strong one, first there in a fight, first there to stick up for you. She'd just watched Alex do that to me and didn't even tell him off. Having the abortion had knocked something out of her. I hoped she could get it back.

'Christmas Eve it is,' Rose said. 'Everyone goes for a Chinese after a night out though, not before.'

'So, we're not everyone. We'll go first.'

'Okay,' Rose was quiet for most of the drive home. I thought she was asleep, we were nearly home when she said, 'Robyn, do you think I'll ever be able to have another baby after…'

'Course you will.'

'Only I was thinking…'

'What?'

The taxi driver lowered the music on his radio.

She didn't answer.

I whispered. 'What, Rose?'

Her eyes were closed. 'It doesn't matter. Don't tell anyone, Robyn, what I've done.'

'I won't. You can tell me anything, honest, I won't tell.'

There was no way I'd be going out for a while after tonight. The way her Rita was blaming me over Simmo, her mum was probably blaming me, too.

I was sure Rose hadn't eaten. That's why she'd got drunk so

easily. When she got that way, her mood went right down. She reminded me of Norm, and how he'd been left to get on with things, leaking out sadness and bad memories, nothing of any good going in to replace it. And the way Alex had behaved; it was shocking the way too much alcohol could change a person, change everything for the worse.

24

Alex came into the shop. I made an excuse, headed to the toilet, stayed in there until he'd gone.

'Has he upset you?' Dot asked.

'Just can't be bothered.'

'He has upset you. He's outside waiting. Said to tell you he wants to see you for a minute.'

'Go on,' Maud said, 'take five minutes while we're slack.'

He was leaning back on the wall. One foot crossed over the other, arms folded; his white shirt dazzling in the sunlight.

He smiled, 'All right?'

'What do you think?'

'Sorry.' He stepped towards me, I stepped back.

'I won't bite.'

'I know you won't.'

'Did you hear what I said?'

'Do anything like that to me again, and I'll frigging murder you, you idiot.'

'What? No need to overreact.'

'I'm not. You shouldn't drink if it turns you into an idiot.'

'I was drunk, I know. I'd been out since early.'

'So?'

'I'm saying sorry.'

'Big deal, it shouldn't have happened in the first place.'

'Yeah, you're making it a big deal the way you're carrying on.'

I walked away. He jumped in front of me.

'Look, I'll start again. I wanted to say sorry, and I wanted to ask if you fancy coming somewhere Sunday afternoon?'

'No.'

'I'll behave, promise.'

'I said no. I like Sundays in.'

'Okay. Tell you what I'll ask you again Friday. See how you feel then. Listen, Robyn, nothing like that will happen again.'

'I don't know you properly. I thought you were all right, and on Saturday I just…if that's what you're really like. I have to get back to work.'

'Come on Sunday you'll see what I'm really like.'

I had no intention of going anywhere with him, but I didn't say it.

On our break, Dot told me she was looking for another job because it was a big mistake getting involved with Ron Fairbrother, and she wouldn't be a laughing stock around this place no more. 'Besides,' she said, 'if I go, they'll need somebody to replace me, so there's more of a chance they'll keep you on.'

'Where will you work?'

'I've got my eye on a couple of places, going to ask around on my day off; don't want to come back here after Christmas.'

I'd miss Dot. There were things about her that made me uncomfortable, but she was nice to me. She held a small cardboard box; covered with Christmas wrapping paper, a little gap in the top. 'What's that?'

'Our tips box, we put it on the counter, share what we get

on Christmas Eve. Last year we ended up with a few quid each. You're entitled to a cut, too. Buy yourself a new dress.'

I thought about Claudia, wondered how she was; planned to go and see her on Saturday, to make sure she was all right.

'How's your preggy mate?'

'Oh, okay. She's not preggy after all.'

'Well that's good. We all make mistakes, some are worse than others.'

Friday, just as I left Waterford's, Alex came out of Man's Gear; he hadn't been in the bakery all week.

'You give any more thought to Sunday? We could meet here, about three?'

'I have my dinner then.'

'Twelve, then, you can get back for your dinner.'

I stopped walking, was about to say no.

But he looked genuinely sorry. 'One chance is all I need. I was an idiot, please?'

Nan said everyone deserved a second chance.

'Robyn? I'm trying here, really want to…'

He was trying. 'All right, I'll see you Sunday.'

He grinned. 'Sunday, we'll meet here, don't let me down now.'

I didn't want to be with him any more, not boyfriend and girlfriend anyway. On Sunday, I'd tell him, from now on we were just friends.

25

There was a Christmas tree up in the corner and boxes of crackers for sale. I hadn't asked Claudia about the marks on her neck, and wouldn't unless she mentioned them.

'Where do you work, Robyn?'

'In a bakery opposite the Adelphi Hotel, it's a six month government scheme.'

'Do you like it there or are you looking for something else?'

'It's all right, you know. Suppose in a way I'd like to be kept on, be sure of a wage, but I'd like to learn how to make clothes, given the choice.'

Claudia walked over to the door and looked through the glass. 'Often, we don't have choices. Events occur and take over; before you know it you're trapped. Once things get dark it's too late to do anything. You hold the whole mess inside, like the clouds stuck up there in the sky, waiting to burst open.'

She tidied the window display, fussed over getting a stiff grey handbag to sit just right on a shelf. Claudia liked to keep things tidy.

'Look, there's an old Singer in the corner. Help me set it up and I'll show you the basics, if you like. Hopefully it still works.'

We lifted the black sewing machine onto a table. Claudia told me the names of all the parts, showed me how to fill the spool with thread and where it slotted into the machine, how to thread the machine, and how to make stitches longer or shorter. She tore a piece of paper out of an address book, doubled it over, sat on my little stool and showed me how to use the wheel at the side of the machine; to make the needle move. The paper slid along the feed dog and came out at the end. I saw a long, straight row of tiny stitches that ran the length of the page.

'You have a go,' she said. 'Make sure your fingers stay well clear of the needle.'

I lifted the foot up, placed the paper beneath it; clunked the foot down, took hold of the little arm on the wheel and turned. The paper started to move, but it went too fast and all wonky. It was tricky trying to move the wheel and keep the paper in position at the same time. I liked the sound and the rhythm it made, liked seeing the fake stitches form on the page.

Claudia said, 'It won't take long for you to master it.' She tore a few more pieces of paper out of her notebook. 'Keep trying until you can sew in a straight line.'

'Thanks, Claudia.'

'Would you like a hot drink?'

'I'd love a tea.'

'You've got time?'

'I'm in no hurry, not out tonight.'

She went into the back.

Claudia had a tape on of Christmas Hymns. *Silent Night* was playing; such a gentle hymn, my favourite to sing. I carried on trying five more times, finally stitching the length of the paper in a straight line, it felt great.

The paintings for sale in the shop were lovely. Boats bobbing on the water with bright yellow sails; a Mexican-looking woman with a long ponytail down her back, picking up an apple from a fruit bowl, paintings of flowers, in vases, in jugs, in meadows. My favourite was the woman. Her dress scooped at the neck; you could see her lace underskirt peeping out of the hem and across her breasts.

Then I spotted the house, a cream house with green shutters and a sloping roof. There was a long path in front of it, and a fence all around with a low gate, painted the same colour as the shutters. A small brown dog sat up straight on the step. If Claudia could be one of these paintings she would be the house. In the front garden there was not a petal out of shape, every blade of grass immaculate, and the shutters on the windows perfectly lined up at the edges.

I showed her the page with my best stitches. She told me I was a fast learner and it made me feel good. The way she gave you her time, and when you spoke to her, she looked you in the eye, really listened to what was being said, and the way she was, not just with me, but with people she served in the shop. I got the feeling that she'd never do you any harm.

'How much is that?'

'What, the painting? Not much, you can have it for fifty pence if you like.'

'I'll take it.'

'Who's it for?'

'Stella, my friend she dreams of having a place of her own. She'll like that for Christmas.'

'She will. Then she can hang it up on her very own wall when she moves. One of the few things in life you can trust, are your dreams.'

Claudia fetched a step-ladder out of the back.

'I'll get it down, Claudia; you shouldn't be climbing up ladders.'

She wrapped it for me while I looked through the video tapes, finding one of Clint Eastwood's on the shelf. Cigar sticking out of the side of his mouth, wearing a poncho and a cowboy hat, pistol held high. The title read: *A Fistfull of Dollars*. I smiled at Claudia. 'I'll take this as well.'

'Who's this one for?'

'Norm, he's a big fan.'

'And Norm is your dad?'

'No, he's another friend.' I didn't want to spoil my time with Claudia by telling her stuff about me, didn't want her feeling sorry for me. That changed things.

'There's a silver pistol over in the children's toy corner, with a roll of caps, might as well give him a prop to use while he watches it.'

'That's a great idea, thanks. He'll get a laugh out of that.'

'The best gifts cost no more than a bit of thought.'

'What's the best gift you've ever had?'

'That's easy. It was a dog. I was eight and my father bought it for me. He was a scruffy little black thing with smelly breath. He had a little white spot on his fur that you could see in the dark. I called him Moonbeam. He never left my side; he even slept in my room. What about you?'

I thought about Nan, and the easy way she had of making you feel special, with a smile, or a meal she'd cooked, or something she did, like hugging you, or our bus rides.

'I don't know. Probably before Nan died, when she said I

could go and live with her. We'd get on a bus to the Pier Head, feed the birds and ride on the ferry, drink hot chocolate from the little kiosk on board.'

'Sounds perfect, it's hard losing someone, your whole landscape shifts, makes you feel powerless for a while, but that changes, you won't feel as lost in a year or so.'

That seemed hard to believe.

About half an hour later, somebody opened the door, a lady with a soaked through umbrella. With her back to us, she shook the rain into the street.

'I'll have to get back. I need to run around the launderette.'

'Why don't I try and get Phil to cover for me next week? I could show you around Southport. You could see my house, if there's time.'

'Okay, yes, I'd like that.'

'I'll meet you at the station, say half ten?'

I picked up the painting and the tape for Norm. 'Okay, see you, thanks.'

Claudia was taking the day off to be with me!

26

Alex knelt down beside a grave; filled an empty carton with water from the tap, then took a sponge and a drop of washing up liquid out of a box. He cleaned the front of the stone where the letters were. 'Grab a sponge and give us a hand.'

I knelt on a grainy rock, Alex handed me a damp, soapy sponge. Brown water trails dripped down the stone, he dabbed them away with a piece of cloth. When it was clean and dry, he spread a sheet of paper across the letters and said, 'This is the best bit.' Using a pencil Alex scratched it from side to side across each letter. Words appeared on the page. 'It's called taking a rubbing,' he said, handing me the pencil. 'Have a go. I'll keep the paper in position.' I scratched the pencil across the page; letters appeared one after another, joining together to form words.

IN MEMORY OF JANE
The wife of Sam Bewley
Who died March 9th 1881
Aged 27 years
In the midst of life we are in death

'That's incredible! So clever, but why doesn't it say anything about her on the stone?'

'It does. Her name's here,' he touched the letters, 'Jane Bewley.'

'It says whose *wife* she was, not who *she* was. Who was Jane? She wasn't just Sam's wife, which is what those words make out. It says nothing about her.'

'We know when she died and how old she was, and we know she was married.'

'But what did she die of? She's not old, twenty-seven. What did she do before she was a wife?'

'There's no room for all that. It's not a book.'

'It doesn't need to be a book, but this, this I think is an insult to her memory. It's more like in memory of the fact that she found a husband.'

'Maybe that was an important thing for a woman to do one-hundred years ago.'

'It probably was, but I wonder if she could sew, or sing. Did she have a job? Did she know how to read? Something that's in memory of somebody should tell us something about them.'

'We're talking about her right now, so she is being remembered.'

'But we don't matter. What if she had a sister? Wouldn't her sister have a memory she could have put on here? Half of the stone is empty.'

'Jesus Christ, I don't know. I haven't thought about it before now.'

'What do you think that means; that last line?' I said.

'In the midst of life we are in death. I think it means, erm, while we're alive we're heading towards death.' He stood up; the knees of his blue jeans stained brown. 'We'll all end up dead, so while we're alive we should remember that, and maybe…' He flicked the soil off with his palms, 'we should use our lives better, if we remember that death's always near, I mean. Does that make sense?'

'It does. But it's scary. If it means while we're living we need to think about death to live a better life. So we'd be constantly thinking about somewhere else, while we're trying to live here. Wouldn't we be better not thinking about death, but imagining living better?'

He laughed, 'I just said that.'

'Sorry, I mean, think about where you are now, not where you're going.'

'If you don't know where you're going you'll get lost.'

'Maybe, but if you don't know where you are in the first place, you could end up going around in circles.'

Alex sounded like he was talking to himself. 'I know how that feels.'

I traced the stone with my palm, it felt cold. 'I wonder who wrote that, putting the words life and death together, like sisters?'

We walked around the cemetery for ages, reading the gravestones. My belly began to rumble. I loved Norm's roast dinners; wanted to make my way there before it got dark. The graveyard was busy, people laying flowers; others had arranged them inside vases. Alex knelt down at a couple of graves, wrote names and dates in a little pad.

'Isn't your nan buried here?'

'No, Ford Cemetery.'

'She got a gravestone?'

'Mum couldn't afford one; there wasn't enough on the insurance policy. She's in an unmarked grave.'

'You can always get a headstone fitted. It can be ten, even

twenty years on, when people have a bit more money, they come back and trace their mum or dad and put a headstone up.'

Then he went all quiet. 'Not exactly a romantic date, this.'

'It's been different, though, good different, thanks.'

He moved in too close to me, I stepped back. 'We can do something you want to do next Sunday, if you like.'

At the gate that led to the main road, I still felt unsure about him, thought about Rose letting Simmo get too close to her, and about the abortion.

'I'd like us to be mates if that's okay? Just mates, for now, I mean you're nice and everything, but-'

'Yeah, mates, I hear you, whatever-'

'Yeah?'

'Yeah.'

He walked in front of me so I couldn't see his face, didn't want him getting the wrong idea.

In the livingroom, Norm was shouting at the telly. It wasn't a Clint Eastwood film, but the news. Somebody had shot John Lennon dead. Somebody in New York was waiting for him outside his apartment block. When he was trying to go home to his son, some man took a gun and killed him.

'Bloody hell,' Norm shouted, 'dirty rotten rat. Lennon never harmed a fly. He's only forty, left his wife and their young son, and his eldest son. What a waste. That's knocked me, that.'

Norm's face was white, 'I saw him, them, on the Cavern in town, we'd never heard nothing like it. That was when he was in the band, when the Beatles were still together. You've got to take your hat off to the four of them, bits of kids they were, grabbed opportunity by the balls and ran with it.'

Norm reached for his whisky, took a swig out of the bottle. 'He had it tough an' all, John. His dad pissed off somewhere, his mother was missing for most of his childhood; some other family member brought him up.'

The news of John's death was on every channel. 'Look at this,' he said, 'now he's dead, he's more alive than ever.'

You'd think by looking at Norm's face, he'd just lost a brother. 'Turn it off, Robyn. Put the records on; there're a couple of John Lennon albums in there somewhere. You heard *Imagine*?'

'Yeah, the other day, I love it.'

'Put that on first.'

The crackly sound of the needle on vinyl; the one two piano chords, John's voice talking about heaven. The words in the song, *Imagine*, about peace and being a dreamer, just beautiful. Norm's words made me think of the words on the gravestone, and John's family: In the midst of life we are in death. They were going to live with John's death in their lives. Like me and Mum thought of Nan, and Dad, who could also be dead, and Rose and her baby. I'd never thought about it that way before, how much death changed the living.

Norm put his favourite John Lennon song on next, a jumpy song, and he knew all the words: *Whatever Gets You through the Night*. I thought how John's childhood was a bit like mine: understood how sad that must have made him feel, being without his parents; craving the attention he never got. I felt pleased that he'd found his music; somebody to love, and, in the end, had his own family.

Norm's eyes were closed, he was singing along to the record. Hopefully my dad, if I ever got to meet him, would be something like Norm.

27

The Southport train stopped at Birkdale. Out of the window, I watched the first soft dusting of snow fall, unexpected because the weather did seem to get warmer. Some of the houses had lights in the windows. It looked magical so early in the morning; red, green and gold lights glowing behind the snowflakes, like delicate spells.

Claudia was on the other side of the barrier. She wore a navy blue skirt suit, white shirt and a small hat tilted over her right eye. She waved when she saw me. 'Good to see you, Robyn.' She took a deep breath in. 'This is great. Doing something different is just what the doctor ordered. Shall we get some breakfast first?'

'Sounds good.'

'There's a quirky little place a few streets away.'

In the café, we sat at a small round table that had pictures of fruit on it. Claudia ordered scrambled eggs on toast and black coffee. 'Same for me, but orange juice instead of coffee,' I said. The snow was falling heavier now, the road and pavement opposite turning white.

'I've moved out of my house, Robyn.'

'You have?'

'Yes, thanks to you.'

'What did I do?'

She cupped the side of her neck with one hand, 'Opened my eyes. Everything you said was true, it wasn't the first time, and he did always, afterwards, apologise. How do you know so much about-?'

'My mum, for years, she was with somebody similar.'

'Everything happens for a reason. I met you for a reason.'

'Where do you live now?'

'On top of a sweet shop not far from here; it's small and cheap, a far cry from what I'm used to but I'm happier.'

'When did you move?'

'Three days ago. He goes to his club Thursday afternoons, I had already packed my stuff, hired a man with a van and left. I've been putting it off for years. That Saturday, the way you reacted, I don't know, maybe it was what you said but you woke me up. I had taken the abuse and simply normalised it.'

I handed her a tissue. 'You've done the right thing.'

'I'm crying because I'm relieved to be out of there.'

'And your job?'

'My job?'

'In the second-hand shop?'

'Oh, that's just voluntary.'

'You don't get paid?'

'No. It's my way of giving something back.'

'He'll come and find you there.'

'He doesn't know I work. I've done that for a year now and he hasn't missed me. Isn't that incredible?'

'It is.'

'He's got his club, his friends…' Her words trailed away, she stared down into her cup, 'The living aren't interested in the dead,' she said. 'And, anyway, I have a small inheritance from my parents that I've never touched.'

For a while we didn't talk; Claudia ordered another drink for us. 'But you've got a point, it won't last for ever,' she said, unbuttoning her jacket. 'I will need to get a little something that pays. I'll be fifty-eight on my next birthday.'

'You don't look fifty-eight.'

'Thanks. A bit late for fresh starts, but still...'

'It's not. Do you have any kids or any family?'

'No kids. I have a sister but she lives in London.'

'Everyone's mad about London,' I said.

Claudia smiled, 'It's a big place, people can disappear easily there.'

'When was the last time you saw your sister?'

'I can't remember. We used to send Christmas and birthday cards but... I can't think. Oh, I actually don't know.'

'You'll be all right, Claudia. I always think that. No matter what happens if you think everything will be all right, it helps.'

'I don't like change; need to know where I'm going. Once I get settled though...'

The lady brought our breakfast. I thickened my eggs in tomato sauce.

'I've let things go, Robyn. Let so many important things go.'

'It can't be helped, sometimes. Other stuff fills up your time.'

'Not any more, I'm free now. What else do you think?'

'What you said before about change. It's part of what happens. I know it's going to come, I don't know when. So stuff scares me but it doesn't surprise me, you've got to keep hoping things will turn out all right. Sometimes change comes and it's a good change.'

'Yes, it is.'

'Sometimes it's easier not to fight, to just give up, but sometimes that's the worst thing you can do.'

'You know, Robyn, you're so young, but I feel like I could talk to you about anything.'

'My problem is I worry too much,' I said. 'I know I do and when I catch myself…'

'You're like me; we both probably need to be a little kinder to ourselves.' Claudia gave me a carrier bag. 'Here, I got you a present.'

It was a large carrier bag with a big heavy box inside.

'Why don't you save it until Christmas morning?'

'I didn't get you anything.'

'Yes you did, because of something you said I've taken the first few steps towards getting my freedom back. I still have to be careful, he's shrewd and he's mean and he'll want revenge. I'm not sure it's safe for you to come and visit me here.'

'You can't let somebody control how you live your life, you've done nothing wrong.'

'I know, maybe it's me getting paranoid. I get the feeling, sometimes, he's watching me.'

It was dark by the time we got back to Southport train station. Claudia stood on the platform, waving at me, stomping her feet, cupping the side of her neck with a palm. Eventually, my train pulled away, she looked so small. I was worried about her.

28

Christmas Eve, I woke to the sound of bacon shishing in the kitchen, looked at the clock; ten to seven.

'Been out already, Norm?'

'Went for the paper; cold as hell out there, you cold?'

'I'm all right.'

'Want egg on toast?'

I remembered Norm's wife died on Christmas Eve, 'I'll do it, Norm. You sit down and eat your own.'

'There's tea in the pot.'

Stella came downstairs, poured herself a cup of tea, big smile on her face. 'We share out our tips today. There's quite a few bob in that box now, can't wait to finish, looking forward to the break.'

'I know, lovely finishing on a Wednesday, and it's really heavy, the box. People are great at this time of year, so generous aren't they?'

Stella nodded, he eyes were all glittery.

When we got to the shop Maud told us we were closing early, four o'clock instead of five. She had a present for all of us. I opened mine on my break. It was a small bottle of Charlie perfume. Dot got the same but Stella got a real silver necklace with an S on it. I hadn't got Maud anything.

Dot sat with me on my break. 'I'm not coming back, Robyn,' she said. 'This is my last day, handed my notice in to Maud last week.'

I stood up, gave Dot a hug. She smelled of Charlie, her favourite perfume and cheese and onion. 'I'll miss you, Dot.'

'I'll come and see you, keep in touch, I promise.'

I knew she wouldn't. Dad never did. If you think about the past too much, it's like part of you gets stuck there, and never comes back.

'You got a new job, Dot?'

She shook her head. 'Not bothered. All my Christmas prezzies are wrapped and paid for. Leaving here means I can start looking properly. You sort things out with Alex?'

'Yeah, it's fine.'

'Got the pill?'

'I'll be all right, we're just mates.'

'Can't tell you young people anything, suppose I was the same at your age; or worse.' She took something out of her bag, handed it to me. 'Here, happy Christmas.'

'Thanks.'

'It's not much.'

'Can I open it?'

'If you like.'

It was a watch with a sky blue face and gold hands; it had a real leather strap. I hadn't got her anything; didn't know they were going to do this. I put it on. 'I love it, thanks. I'll give you your prezzie after dinner.'

'Don't go mad,' Dot said. 'Twelve quid should easily cover mine.'

I laughed. 'That's a shame. I was thinking of spending twenty quid on you. My bus fares back to work and everything.'

'That's right, take out a bank loan, champagne will do. A week walking to work will do you the world of good. Come here, Robyn,' she hugged me tight, spoke into my hair. 'Out of them all in here I'll miss you most, you're a little cracker.'

My eyes were tearing up.

On my dinner break I asked Maud for my wages; ran across to Lewis's, bought Maud a cerise pink chiffon scarf and Dot a red leather purse. I put ten pence in it for luck. Alex was standing on the step of Man's Gear.

'Been busy?'

'Not really, you?'

'It's dead. I've sold one pair of Levi's and two Fred Perry jumpers all morning. Going out tonight?'

'Not sure.'

'Cindy's is tickets.'

'You're messing?'

'Honest. Tickets only, didn't think you knew.' He slid his hand in his back pocket handed me an envelope.

I opened the envelope; two tickets for Cindy's.

'For you and Rose.'

'Ahh that's lovely, so thoughtful.'

'See you in there?'

'Okay; and thanks.'

I turned around, ran back over to Lewis's, bought Alex a grey crew neck jumper reduced to half price. I just hoped Rose hadn't got me anything. I'd only just been paid and was nearly skint, still needed to give Norm my keep. At least we had our tips to come.

After work Dot gave me another hug. 'I'll call in and see you in January,' she said. Then she disappeared inside a queue at the bus stop opposite. It made me think, how nobody stayed around for long.

When me and Stella got off the bus, we called into the chippy for our tea.

Norm came in drunk just after us. He'd got off work early, went to the pub with the men he worked with, in no time, he was snoring his head off upstairs. We ate our chippy tea in front of the telly.

'Nearly five pounds each tips,' Stella said, chip between her teeth.

'I'm made up with that,' I said.

'I'm putting all of it away, and half of my wages.'

'Aren't you out tonight?'

'Got a bottle of red and the telly's great.'

My plate was empty, I'd ate too much, felt tired, didn't feel like going out, pulled the two tickets for Cindy's out of their envelope. If Rose didn't knock, I'd stay in with Stella.

Stella shook me awake. Rose was sitting on the settee all dressed up. 'We might not get in, tickets only our Rita said.'

I'd had a lovely sleep. Felt refreshed, handed Rose the two tickets Alex gave me. She stood up and squashed my chest with her hug. I ran a bath then got dressed as fast as I could.

Downstairs, Rose was drinking vodka with Stella. 'Thought you weren't drinking?'

'It's Christmas,' Stella said. 'She's having a little Christmas drink.'

'I'm trying to get Stella to come.'

'I'm not going out in that, it's pissing down, and you'll never get a taxi home tonight, they charge double.'

She was right, there wasn't much point. 'Why don't we just stay in?' I asked.

Rose stared at me, smiled and said, 'Okay, why not?'

'What a shitty Christmas Eve,' Stella said, looking out the window at the rain.

'I've had worse,' Rose said. 'Last Christmas Eve, my dad lost his wages, when he was out with the lads from work. Mum had no money to buy the shopping. He came home about three o'clock in the afternoon and realised his wallet was gone. We had beans on toast last Christmas for dinner.'

We couldn't help it; the look on Rose's face when she told us. Me and Stella laughed and laughed. Stella got us all another vodka and coke, got comfy again on the settee.

'Go on Robyn, you go next. What's the shittiest Christmas Eve you've ever had?'

I took a sip of my drink. 'I remember one Christmas Eve, my mum got drunk in the afternoon. She took me food shopping. There was a man dressed as Santa in the corner of the supermarket, giving out presents to the kids. Mum pushed to the front of the queue, sat on Santa's knee, pulled his beard down and kissed him right on the lips. When she finally got up off his knee, his beard had fallen to the floor and all the kids were screaming.'

Rose and Stella were howling.

We stopped laughing. 'My all-time shittiest ever Christmas Eve, was when…is when…' Stella stopped, downed her drink and walked into the kitchen. Rose looked at me but said nothing. I followed Stella into the kitchen. She poured herself another drink.

'I hate Christmas,' she said. 'It's awful. And tonight is the shittiest Christmas Eve I've ever had. I'm so glad you and Rose stayed in. I don't think I've ever felt this low. Have another drink with me?'

Then I thought about Stella's prezzie, the picture of the house, ran upstairs and cleaned the frame with wet cotton wool, dried it off with toilet paper. It looked much brighter.

Downstairs, I asked Stella to close her eyes.

'Why?' she said.

'Just do it.'

I grabbed the painting from the hall. 'Okay, keep your eyes closed but hold out your hands. I let it rest across her palms, keeping tight hold. 'Okay, open them.'

Stella screamed when she saw it. 'Ahh. It's sweet that, look at the little dog, and the house is-'

'Let's see,' Rose said.

'In a minute, Rose, I'm looking at it a bit longer. I take back what I said before. This is one of the best Christmases, ever.'

Later, Rose said she'd get a taxi home, but Stella told her to stay because taxis were too dear around Christmas. After a while, I went up to bed, left Stella and Rose to chat; tiptoed past Norm's room, even with the door shut, you could still hear him snoring.

Next morning, I didn't get up until eleven. Norm was up but Stella was still in bed. He told me Rose had gone home around ten.

'I'll start the dinner now, Robyn, fancy giving me a hand? We could share a bottle of Guinness?'

Nan loved Guinness.

'Okay, pass me the veg.'

'Did Stella have a late one last night?'

'Think so.'

'I'll go and put the records on low; John Lennon all right?'

'John Lennon's great. Put *Imagine* on.' I took the knife out of the drawer, filled the bowl with warm water, plopped the spuds in; thought about my mum, wondered what she'd be doing today. And Dad, God only knew where he was. Then I thought about last Christmas, in Nan's, just me and Nan. No turkey but lamb chops done in special onion gravy, we drenched our dinner in it; mopped up what was left with crusty bread and butter.

Imagine was playing, Norm was singing, the water turned murky from the soil. I watched my tears plop one after the other into the bowl. We let the music bleed all over us, let somebody else's words form on our lips.

'Better than listening to Christmas carols,' he said, lifting a huge turkey out of the oven. 'Not done yet. I'll put Fred back in the oven, eh? Soon as they unloaded this beauty I bagzied it, there'll be plenty over for sandwiches tonight and some great films on, Robyn. You seen *Wonderful Life*?'

'No.'

I blinked the tears away, straightened myself out; couldn't think too much about things, like my first Christmas without Nan. I thought of the thank you card she got last Christmas, from the community centre, for knitting loads of baby cardigans, and the hamper; and her clapping with delight, carefully unwrapping the cellophane, lifting each item like they were made of glass. 'Isn't this something, Robyn?' she'd said, 'such a kind thing for them to do.'

Today had to be tough on Norm, without Stella's mum; and he must have still missed his first wife. I wasn't the only one having a shitty Christmas.

'Is it good?'

'Better than good; we'll watch it later. I think you'll like it, James Stewart.' He was holding a bottle of Guinness.

'How about a Christmas morning drink?'

'Nah, Norm, I...'

'Come on, just a little one? Let's enjoy it, I don't care what you say, we're all better off this year than that poor sod in there, singing. There'll be no prezzies getting opened in his place today.'

'But they've got his music, Norm, there's a bit of him in that. Maybe they're listening to *Imagine*.'

'Yeah, suppose he's still living in a way, through his music.'

'You know what, Norm, you're right.'

'How about that drink?'

'Go on then. Not Guinness, though, any Babycham left?'

While he poured the drinks, I ran upstairs and got his gift.

'For you, Norm.'

He clunked his glass down on the table. 'What's all this?'

'A prezzie, open it.'

He handed me my drink, took the gift and kissed me on the cheek. 'You shouldn't have.'

Norm opened it and smiled. 'That's so thoughtful, love. I didn't buy any this year, didn't think, sorry.'

'You're making the dinner, Norm, can't give a better prezzie than food. Your roasts are ace.' I took a sip of my drink. Norm picked his up, clinked my glass. 'Merry Christmas, Robyn,' he said.

'Merry Christmas to you, Norm,' I said, and I meant it.

We heard music playing loud in front of the house; looked out of the kitchen window. Two kids carrying a gigantic music system, speakers held high up to their ears.

'What the hell's that?' Norm asked.

'A ghetto blaster.'

'Never heard of it; sounds like a new government regeneration policy.'

We laughed and it felt good.

Upstairs, taking Claudia's gift out, I sat on the edge of the bed and tore off the paper. It was a brand new sewing machine.

I hoped she was okay, that her Christmas would go well, thought maybe she could come here for tea soon, meet Norm. She'd like him for sure.

29

1981

That first Monday of a brand new year, Norm didn't get up for work. He said he had bad pains in his belly, was taking the day off. Stella made him a cup of tea before we ran for the bus. When we got back from work it was still on his bedside table, untouched. I got him a glass of water, he half sat up and sipped it. He didn't look well; said it was probably a bug and he just needed sleep. Stella ran around to the owner of Bexlin's butchers to let him know.

Norm wouldn't let Stella call a doctor out. 'I'll be dancing again by Saturday night,' he said, 'you'll see.'

Friday came, Stella looked worried. She said, 'If he doesn't get out of bed on Saturday, there's something really wrong and I'm getting the doctor, with or without his permission.'

I woke up on Saturday morning and heard Stella crying downstairs. She was sitting on the arm of the settee in her Waterford's overall. 'What's wrong?'

'It's Norm.'

'What?'

'Go upstairs and try and wake him. I can't get him to move.'

I ran up to his room. There was a bad smell in there. On the bedside table, three full cups of tea with skin on the top. From the bedroom door I shouted his name. 'Norm, Norm, you okay?' I walked over to his bed. He was a pale grey colour. His hands were cold, like Nan's were. I shouted for Stella to come up. She stood in the doorway, tears all over her face.

'He's dead isn't he? I should've got a doctor.'

'But you didn't know.'

'He was so lovely, Robyn.'

Norm's foot stuck out of the covers at the bottom of the bed. I could see a small round bruise in the centre where he'd been tying his laces too tight. I lifted the blanket up to cover the mark.

Me and Stella held each other tight. 'I know, he was the best,' I said.

Downstairs, I made a pot of tea. We sat in the livingroom and said nothing for a long time. The tea went cold so I made another one and handed Stella her cup.

'What're we gonna do? We need to tell somebody. Who do we tell?'

I thought about the morning me and Betty found Nan. 'We need to ring a doctor and you'll need to contact your mum, everything else will just happen.'

Stella looked over at the record player, 'Not yet, then. Let's put his records on, before everything happens. You think that's an all right thing to do?'

I stood up, switched on the record player; took John Lennon's LP out of the sleeve. 'Whatever you want, Stella,' I said. 'Norm loved his music. I think he'd like that.'

Stella put her tea down. 'He would like that. I'll open his

room door wide, turn that up a bit louder, Robyn, maybe he can still hear it. At least he's in his own home, his own bed.'

When Nan died, if I'd have known, it would've have been better if we'd have been doing something she loved. Sitting on a bench down at the Pier Head watching the boats, feeding the birds, or singing along to an old song, or me reading her a chapter from a book, but Death isn't like that, it doesn't arrive all singing and all dancing, nor does it turn up by invitation, it comes inside a whisper, or a faulty choice, or a creak in the floorboards, nearly always while you're busy thinking about something else.

30

Jean, Stella's mum, looked like a film star, with short honey-blonde curls and dark eyes. She wore a tight grey pencil skirt, high heels and a red pussy bow blouse. She sorted everything out. The doctor, the death certificate, the funeral, Norm's clothes, his stuff out of his room. But not his LPs. Stella said they stayed where they were.

One week after Norm's funeral, Jean said, 'Me and Siggy want to talk to you girls. Monday about half six, we'll call around.'

Siggy was a thin man with a skinny throat. 'Have you met my boyfriend?' Jean said to me.

Stella let out a, 'Ha!'

He talked about bills and how we couldn't keep things going on our wages alone. He said all this before he asked us what days we worked and how much wages we got. 'And anyway,' the sound of his voice hard as pebbles, 'Jean's name is on the rent book, and she's been and paid the rent up to date, so this place is now rightfully hers.'

Jean smiled, flung her arm around his shoulder, 'Ours, mine and Siggy's.'

Under her breath, Stella said, 'Pair of cunts.'

'Grab us a fork, girl,' Siggy said to me, opening up his tray from the chippy.

In the kitchen drawer, I searched for the fork with the sticking up prong.

Back in the livingroom, Jean said, 'Not that we'd kick you out or anything…'

She fixed her eyes on Stella. 'That was a burst appendix. Poor Norm, he must have been in agony. If a doctor was called sooner, there's a chance he would've lived.'

Siggy stuck the fork in his pie stuffed it in his mouth and swore.

Nobody said anything for ages; then Jean looked at Stella. 'Never mind; you wasn't to know, any chance of offering your poor mum a cuppa?'

Stella said nothing.

'I'll make it,' I said. We closed the door over and went into the kitchen.

'Cheeky cow,' Stella said, while I filled up the kettle. She snatched it off me, banged it onto the oven. 'If she'd have still been here none of this would have happened. What she forgets is; he was in agony because of what that slag did to him. Only reason I'm keeping my gob shut is because me and you have nowhere to live. She's up to something, Robyn.'

Stella listened at the livingroom door to Jean and Siggy. She called me over.

Stella's mum said, 'We'll have to give them jobs.'
Siggy said, 'We'll do the cooking.'
'Get that pen and paper, do a list.'
'For each day.'
'Windows once a week.'
'What day?'

'And bedding and bathrooms.'
'Give them to Robyn.'
'More time on her hands.'
'Saturday: bathrooms. Write that down.'
'We'd have to check them.'
'Don't want sloppiness.'
'Earn their keep.'
'And pay up.'
'Can't have the music too loud.'
'Write that down.'
'How much keep each week?'
'Five or seven?'
'Seven-seven's fair.'
'We can't run this place on fresh air.'
'We've got bills to pay. Seven pounds each. Write that down.'
'Windows: what day?'
'Sunday.'
'They've been getting away with murder.'
'No sense of responsibility.'
'No common sense. No respect.'
'For anybody, that'll change.'
'It's not going to be easy.'
'Young people today.'
'They should be grateful.'
'It's for their own good.'
'No bringing fellas home.'
'No. Write that down.'
'Not under this roof.'
'They can stay at the fella's place.'
'They'll get pregnant, lose their jobs.'
'No staying out.'

'No staying out. What time in?'

'Weekends: eleven. No staying out on any night. Write that in capital letters.'

'More trouble than they're worth.'

'Wouldn't get many people like us doing this.'

'No.'

'They should be grateful.'

'They should.'

'If they want to be treated like adults…'

'Let them see the list.'

'They should sign it.'

'Like an agreement.'

'From now on things will be done our way.'

'Our way or the highway.'

They both giggled.

Stella looked at me, crinkled up her eyes. She turned away, went upstairs to her room. Once I'd taken the tea into Jean I followed her upstairs. 'I'm not frigging staying here.'

'Stella?'

'I'll move back in with my dad. Even though I hate it, two of my brothers live there and the three of them argue all the time. But I've got no choice, can't afford my own place yet. What about you, can you ask somebody?'

My heart shifted into a place that felt wrong. I shuddered, thinking about the bench in St John's Gardens, wished I knew where my dad was.

'I'll sort it.'

Next day on my dinner, I took a walk. People wrapped up in

scarves and hats. Little kids with navy blue, or black balaclavas, to keep their faces warm.

Earlier this morning, there was a homeless man crouched inside the shop doorway. His hands were shaky and he had dry blood on his lips. He looked so cold. His hair was grey and wiry and I gazed into his eyes for longer than I should've. They had a shift in them, wild and soft, a hurricane and a breeze, something delivered by the wind.

'You okay, mate?' I said.

'Spare some change?' he asked, holding out his hand.

I pressed my dinner money into his palm.

'Thanks, love.'

He shuffled down towards Lewis's. I could have been sitting there, I thought; if it wasn't for the kindness of strangers. And I felt like a little bit of me had betrayed Nan, her telling me to never rely on anybody but yourself. Would she be disappointed in me, if she could see how I was living? Relying on other people, with only money to offer as an apology for barging into their lives? I could still end up homeless, despite everything, that person sleeping in a doorway, going to buy a cup of tea with money he'd begged, could still very easily be me.

31

After the funeral, it was clear Stella wasn't going to last much longer in Norm's, spending most of her time, when she wasn't working, in her room. We got one meal a day, our tea. Yesterday, it was freezing cold in the shop; we couldn't keep the heat in with customers leaving the door open all the time. When we got to Norm's, Siggy had made us a chopped pork salad and two slices of thin bread.

When Siggy left the room I swapped my tomatoes for a slice of Stella's bread; like secretly helping out a fellow prisoner.

I didn't want to go to Edinburgh, hoped to be kept on at Waterford's. Maud said last time she spoke to Mr Fairbrother, the situation looked hopeful. She told me to keep my fingers crossed. Maybe me and Stella could get our own place? She was dead easy to be with and she had a plan. But there was no way we could afford everything between us.

It wasn't fair on her; she wanted me to try and find a place to live by the end of this week; didn't want to give one penny more to those two leeches. It was Tuesday, and I still hadn't come up with anything. Rose asked her mum for me but she said there was no room.

Alex was standing on the step of Man's Gear, both hands in his pockets.

'You okay?' he said when I got closer.

'I've been better.'

'Come in, the boss isn't here today, he's gone to Manchester, we need new stock.'

I checked my watch, 'Okay.'

Inside the shop there weren't many clothes on the rails. Alex started shuffling the hangers around. 'We got hammered here Saturday, with the sales. Why didn't you turn up at Cindy's? I was searching for you.' He stopped talking and looked at me. 'What's with the face?'

'I'm all right.'

He got me a chair, told me to sit down, 'Tell me,' he said.

'Sorry about Cindy's. Norm's dead.'

'Norm?'

'Norm, he's, well, was like Stella's second dad. He let me stay in his, but he's dead now and he was…thing is, I think if we'd have known what we were dealing with, we might have been able to…'

'No, don't cry, I'm sorry.'

I wiped my face. 'Anyway, I have to find somewhere else to live.'

'And your mum and dad?'

'My mum lives in a pub in Edinburgh, don't know where my dad is.'

Alex was quiet for a minute.

'Maybe I could…?'

'What?'

'There's me, and my dad, he's a bit quirky…'

'Quirky?'

'You know…'

'I don't know. What're you saying?'

'There's a box room full of junk. It used to be my room, but I got the bigger room once my brother moved out. There's a single bed.'

'Really, and your dad wouldn't mind, I can pay keep.'

Alex stared at me. 'That'll impress him, and he'll be made up you're working. Don't get your hopes up, he's a moody bugger and will probably say no.'

'And your mum?'

'She moved out years ago.'

'Oh, I'm sorry.'

He shrugged.

Back in work, Stella looked relieved when I told her Alex might have a spare room. 'Sorry to push you,' she said, 'I can't stay there much longer; both of them sleeping in Norm's bed, not even buying a new mattress. It's making me sick. I mean for God's sake, how could they?'

I'd thought about that; thought of Norm, and how he died in that bed. Lovely Norm, who tried to tie himself into this world by his shoelaces, I imagined him sitting in the little chair in the corner of his room, watching them at night; and getting a nark on with me and Stella for letting them sleep in his bed. I couldn't wait to move out myself.

'You wanna see the poky little cupboard I've got. You can't even fit a wardrobe in. I'll be living out of carrier bags.'

Wednesday morning Alex was waiting outside the shop. 'Dad

said it's all right for you to stay. He's clearing the box room out tomorrow.'

'Did he just say yes?'

'He asked a few questions. I told him what you told me.'

'And he said yes?'

'He said, see how it goes.'

'Is he usually easy going like that?'

I heard laughter, roughly trembling in his throat. 'I told him you work most of the time so he won't see you. I told him you're on a government scheme and we're mates.'

'Well, we are. Thanks, Alex. Tell your dad thanks. Stella can move out now. She'll be made up.'

The carrier bags we took from Norm's were inside the little cupboard in Waterford's. Stella had one bag full of his LPs. 'They're not getting their filthy mitts on these,' she said. 'Choose one, Robyn. Norm would want you to.'

'You sure?'

She nodded.

Looking back, I was sorry I didn't say yes to Nan's cross and chain when Mum asked. 'Can I have the John Lennon?'

'There's two here.' She took them out of the bag and handed them to me, one of the albums was called, *Walls and Bridges*.

Maud saw the bags and asked Stella what was going on. Stella made up a story about taking them to a second-hand shop. When Maud saw the picture of the house and the little dog she said, 'I'll have that. Don't be giving something as good as that away to a charity shop.'

Stella looked at me for help. 'She's not giving that away, are you Stella?'

'No.'

'Then why's it here?'

'She bought it herself, from a second-hand shop.'

Maud shook her head. 'The stuff people throw away these days; treasures, probably got a family history behind it that picture.'

I remembered, with everything going on, I hadn't seen Claudia since before Christmas.

32

Alex's dad opened the front door that hung too far down to the left. He dropped his book of matches onto the scarred wooden floorboards, I picked them up. He stepped aside for me to enter, my shoes squeaked against the grooves. Alex sloped off to the toilet while his dad showed me the room. At the top of the staircase, an old dressing table with a cracked mirror blocked the way. You had to squeeze past it. If Nan was here she'd say, *seven years bad luck,* make him cover it with a sheet. On the landing there were loads of cardboard boxes stacked up on top of each other, full of outdated newspapers, and old bicycle parts.

He didn't show me the kitchen or the livingroom, they were rooms I probably wouldn't be in much. His eyes sat too far apart from each other, his hair, grey and slippery and his hands were huge compared to his small body. Huge hands to dig graves with. His face was a serious face, a face that suited waiting in graveyards for the dead.

In the bedroom there was a wardrobe with a mirror inside. A couple of floorboards were loose and I thought of a film I saw once, on Rose's telly, about a man with thick glasses who murdered women and hid them under the floorboards.

'I'll have to fix that,' Alex's dad said; then he turned and left.

I took my dresses from Claudia's shop out of the bags and hung them up; slid the John Lennon under the bed; everything else stayed in the carrier bags, just in case. I was lucky compared to Stella, who didn't even have a wardrobe.

He was standing in the doorway. I jumped backwards, knocked a little clock onto the floor.

'Sorry,' I said, picking it up.

He took it from me and checked it.

If he ever smiled, I thought, it was not because he liked to, but because he'd been forced to. He looked around the room, 'It's small.'

'It's fine.'

He turned away from me.

'What's your name?'

'Derek.'

'Okay.'

'I'll let you finish.' He closed the door tight. Then I knew why he was being funny with me. I opened the room door, shouted after him, 'Don't know if Alex told you–'

'He told me. When the time comes, don't want any nonsense happening here, not in this house.'

He stopped walking down the stairs. I took money out of my jeans pocket and held it out to him. 'My keep, I can pay keep.'

'That's something I suppose,' he said. 'Just make sure there's no nonsense here, no abusing the favour. My lad's salt of the earth.'

Back inside the room I opened the window; heard mournful howls coming from a dog, nearby. It was too dark to see very much so I closed it again, pulled back the cream sheets and got into bed with my clothes on. Something about the way Derek was with me didn't add up, his coldness frightened me. I was going to keep out of his way.

Next morning, I checked the time on my watch, ten to seven, opened the bedroom window, it was light outside. I could see washing lines in backyards. Most of the washing lines were empty, except for Alex's; a couple of blue towels and a striped shirt. A black cat sat on the wall, green eyes looking up at me. I shivered, shut the window and got back into bed. Then I remembered: Saturday.

Edging past the boxes along the landing to the bathroom, I forgot to get my toothbrush from Norm's. I had a wash, squeezed out toothpaste onto my finger, rubbed it across my teeth and gums. Back in the bedroom, I got ready to go out. Alex came out of his bedroom. 'You sleep okay?'

'Yes, thanks,' I lied.

'Where're you off?'

'Southport.'

'What for?'

'To see my friend.'

'You out tonight?'

'I'll ask Rose.'

'What time will you be back?'

'Don't know, you in work?'

'Yeah, you're lucky, every Saturday off.'

'Alex, your dad told me he doesn't want any nonsense from me while I'm here. What does he mean?'

He shrugged. 'You'll have to ask him.'

It was only a short walk from Alex's to the train station. I loved the train ride to Southport. Everything about it was so relaxing. The clickety-clack sound it made, the gentle way it rocked from side to side, and the view out of the huge windows; this morning the train was half-empty. I had four seats and a table all to myself.

Looking out of the window, I was thinking about Mum, who still thought I was in Rose's.

There must be somebody else with a spare room; staying with Alex and his dad for too long would be torture. I really loved living in Norm's. My head hurt with it all. I tried to think about Dot, wondered if she was still married, and had found a new job.

Claudia was serving a woman buying a grey wool coat. 'Won't be a minute,' she said. 'Take a seat.'

There were a couple of new paintings on the wall, paintings of flowers; not as nice as Stella's house and dog, though. There was only one other customer in the shop. A tall man, wearing a grey checked flat cap. When Claudia had finished serving, she sat down next to me.

'How was your Christmas?'

I thought about helping Norm with the Christmas dinner and giving Stella and Norm their presents. 'It was great, thanks. How was yours?'

'Quiet. But that's how I like it. And peaceful, I got through four novels. If I'd have known you were coming I'd have booked the day off. My flat looks a bit better now.'

'Thanks for the sewing machine, I love it.'

'You're welcome.'

'I wasn't sure if I'd make it today, had loads of stuff happening…'

'You don't have to explain, I understand. Are you in a hurry to get back?'

'Not really.'

'If you hang around for a bit, Phil's coming in to let me go on my dinner. I can take a tad longer, if he's not busy, show you the flat.'

'Okay.'

'I've had no nice dresses in. I've been looking for you.'

'I have plenty of dresses. I've come to see you, you been okay?'

'Much better.'

'You look happier.'

'Thanks.'

The man with the flat cap was at the counter holding a black tie. Claudia served him then went into the back to make us a cup of tea. The man stared at her as she walked away.

'That lady,' he said to me, 'is her name Emily?'

'No, it's Claudia,' I said.

'Claudia?'

'Yes,' I smiled.

He didn't smile back.

He turned away and walked straight out of the shop.

The morning passed quickly, Claudia got busy, she asked me to help her serve for a bit. When Phil came in, he told her to take a couple of hours for her dinner. Claudia grabbed her coat and we flew out of the door; along Lord Street, to a bakery to buy sandwiches. I bought a toothbrush in a chemist. Claudia was in good spirits, chatty and smiling; talking about the man who owned the sweet shop, Mr Seger, 'He's so lovely,' she said, 'can't do enough to help me.'

It was while we were waiting to cross the busy road to Claudia's flat, that I saw him again, the man with the flat cap standing in a phone box. The lights changed and we crossed over. When we got to the other side of the road I asked Claudia if there was a café near so we could sit for a minute. She took me to a place called Carmines. I found an empty table while Claudia ordered two teas. She sat down opposite me.

'Claudia, I might be wrong about this, but I think somebody's following you.'

The rosy colour on her skin turned milky-grey. 'Tell me why you think that?'

'This man, in the shop when you went to make the tea, asked me if your name was Emily. I said no, her name's Claudia. I mean it could be nothing, but I just saw him again, while we were crossing over, and he was in the phone box, talking to somebody, staring across at you.'

Claudia took in a big breath; then let it out in a fast tremble.

'Do you think somebody might be following you?'

'It's possible.'

'Who?'

'He could be a private detective.'

'But that only happens-'

'In films?'

'Yes.'

'Not if your husband's a police inspector.'

'And your husband is?'

'Yes, so he's in the game of hunting things down. I should have known it wouldn't be this easy.'

'What're you going to do?'

'I can't go back to the shop.'

'Ever again?'

'Ever again.'

'Is he doing this because he wants you back?'

'He's probably doing this because he wants me dead.'

I looked into her eyes. They'd lost all their sparkle. She was scared. I put my hand over her hand. 'Don't worry. He knows about the shop but he mustn't know where you live.'

'Of course he couldn't know where I live. After all, I've been using the back way in and out. Nobody knows it's there.'

'Still, you can't take any chances-'

'You believe me? You believe me when I tell you I think he could kill me?'

'Why wouldn't I?'

'I think of it, of saying it, and I think people will laugh.'

I thought about the bruises on Claudia's neck. 'I'm not laughing, Claudia. There's nothing funny about being scared of a bully.'

'No, but not everybody will react the way you have. I can't go to the police. They'll laugh. They all know who he is, the reputation he has and they won't believe a word I say.'

A girl not much older than me brought our tea. I picked up the teapot and poured us both a cup. We didn't speak for a long time then Claudia said, 'I need to get my things out of the flat and leave. It's only a matter of time now. He'll find me soon. I take what you saw today as a warning, Robyn. I need to get out of Southport.'

'Do you want me to come to the flat with you?'

'Would you?'

'Of course.'

'I want to get a few of my things, jewellery, my mother's wedding ring, bank books, important things, really. It won't take me long. Maybe it's not safe for you to come?'

I tried not to let Claudia sense how frightened I was for her. 'I'll come with you.'

'Are you sure?'

'I'm sure.'

We finished our tea, made our way to Claudia's flat.

33

On our way, I kept my eyes open for the man wearing the flat cap. Looking in every doorway and every bus stop but I didn't see him. Then I thought Claudia's going to leave the home she's made because I told some man her name, and spotted him looking over at her. Maybe I was wrong. Maybe it was all a coincidence.

Claudia led me up a side street; slotted her key in the lock of a dark green door. We rushed along a narrow passageway, towards a flight of stairs. Once we were upstairs, she snatched a large travel bag out of a cupboard, stuffed papers and clothes inside. She was fast, knew what drawers to tip out, and what drawers to leave alone. The place started to look like a burglar had ravaged it.

'You sure about this, Claudia, I'm not sure any more? What if I was wrong? What if he's not looking for you at all? You're leaving a place you just turned into a home. I feel terrible about this. Is there a way of finding out if he's onto you for sure, before you pack up and leave?'

'There is a way of finding out for sure. But it'll be too late. By then you'll be hearing about it on the six o'clock news.'

Claudia pointed at the dresser, her hand shaking: 'Second

draw down, my jewellery box. Leave the box; tip the contents into the bag, hurry. If that man's followed us here, it won't take long for him to report back.'

She opened a drawer in the side of a coffee table, grabbed a bunch of notes; closed the drawer with her knee. There was a knock on Claudia's room door. We both stopped what we were doing. Claudia was on her knees on the floor. She closed her eyes. Somebody knocked again, louder this time. She opened her eyes, pressed a finger up to her lips for me to stay quiet. I felt my neck going hot, wanted to run behind the settee and hide. We waited. Heard the sound of footsteps going back downstairs; Claudia sat with her back against the coffee table, eyes wide.

She left it for a few minutes, picked up the travel bag and her handbag, listened at the door. When she opened it, there was nobody there. 'It might have just been Mr Seger, the landlord,' she whispered.

Inside the taxi, she told the driver to go to the train station. It was once we arrived at the station, another taxi pulled up behind us, and a tall, bald-headed man, wearing a brown leather jacket and brown trousers, stepped out. He paid the driver through the window, marched over to Claudia, grabbing her by the arm.

She panicked, stumbled backwards against a woman carrying a baby in her arms. 'Watch out, you stupid cow,' the woman screamed.

Claudia apologised, pulled herself free from the man I now knew was her husband. He grabbed her again.

'Where do you think you're going you stupid, sneaky bitch?' He dragged her and the bag away from the main door, towards the road, Claudia was shouting, pulling away from him.

I ran over.

'Let go of her,' I said, 'right now.'

He stopped. 'Beat it,' he said to me. He put his face up close to Claudia's, 'You're coming with me,' he said, like everything had already been decided.

'Graham, stop this, for God's sake, I'm not coming back with you, ever again, give me my bag?'

He had his hand clamped around the back of her neck. 'You know what kind of a Christmas I had, on my own? You selfish cow, won't last five minutes without me, you stupid-'

I snatched the travel bag from his hand.

He struggled, lunging at me while trying to hold onto Claudia. He shoved me to the floor, I bashed my knee; it started bleeding.

I shouted, 'Help, somebody!'

Running towards the ticket office, I shouted louder. 'Help us, somebody, quickly my friend's in trouble.'

When I turned back around, there was a moment between what I expected to see, and what I saw. Claudia was falling forwards into the road.

I felt the screech of the car's brakes as well as hearing them, the roar of tyres on gravel. Somebody passing by screamed. I couldn't move, helpless, hoping that the driver would stop before he crushed her.

Everything felt soft and crumbly, like even the pavements were breaking down. I let out a sob, cried out her name, watched the vehicle as it finally stopped about an inch away from her head, front bumper hovering; lovely Claudia, sprawled out and helpless, face down in the road.

A guard came running around the corner; almost pushed me over. One of the men selling tickets left his till and ran over to the roadside. The man behind the wheel of the car held his face in his hands.

'What's your game?' the guard asked Claudia's husband.

'Fuck off, I'm a police officer. I'll have you behind bars if you don't mind your own business.'

I ran into the road, helped Claudia up, her forehead was bleeding.

'He pushed me, Robyn,' she whispered. 'Once you left to get help, he pushed me into the road. Get me as far away from that bastard as you can, please.'

Her whole body was shaking. 'Let's get to the platform. Hold onto my arm.'

I heard the guard laughing, 'Oldest one in the book that, mate, a police officer my eye, and no need for the vulgar language.'

Graham shouted, 'You're an idiot,' elbowed the guard in the face. Another guard blew his whistle, two men ran over, forcing Claudia's husband to the floor. We ducked under the barrier. I could see one last person boarding the Liverpool train. We rushed inside the cabin, the doors whooshed behind us. The sound of a final whistle, the most wonderful thing I'd heard all day. The train pulled away and we left Southport behind for good.

Claudia caught her breath, arranged her bags on the empty seats. 'What an absolute bastard he really is, and he'll never get an opportunity to do anything like that to me again.'

'As long as you're okay. We forgot to buy our tickets.'

She was laughing and crying at the same time. 'It doesn't matter; we can pay at the other side. You're funny, Robyn, worrying about the tickets.'

'Look at your tights, they're all laddered, and you're bleeding.'

'I'll get a new pair, it's all right; it's going to be all right. No tickets, no tights but still alive, eh? Look, you're bleeding, too, you poor thing.' But the laughter had gone and she was crying now. Tears racing all down her face, making dark tracks through her powder.

'Dragging you into my mess, I'm so sorry, you're still a child.'

Claudia gave me a tissue for my knee, I took another, dabbed away the blood on her forehead, she didn't look back, didn't say another word; kept her eyes closed all the way to Liverpool.

I waited downstairs in the reception area. Once she'd settled we took a walk around. I showed her Waterford's bakery, which was right across the road from the Adelphi, where she was staying. We walked down to the Pier Head. Claudia looked out across the Mersey for ages.

We watched one ferry boat go out, just as another was coming in. They passed each other and blew their horns. Claudia said she'd get a good night's sleep, and know what to do in the morning, once her head had cleared.

'I'm sorry for putting this on you, Robyn.'

'It's nothing,' I said.

We stood there for a long time, looking out across the Mersey, I felt closest to Nan when I was down here.

'There's something about being by water, the rush of it, as if it drinks all the bad thoughts away.'

Claudia looked down at the water while she spoke. 'I've waited a long time for this day, imagined it so often. Looking out at all of this space makes me realise, I threw myself away in that relationship.'

She was talking to herself more than me; her small hands gripped the railings. 'Being with the wrong person makes you feel more than alone, because you don't let yourself think about it. And it gets to the point where you've swallowed so much of yourself down, you start to drown inside.' She looked across at me. 'Be sure, Robyn, before you give your love away to anyone.'

'I don't know how you can be sure?'

'Graham, my husband, was a police officer when I met him, I felt like I'd been given a ticket to freedom. I thought he'd protect me from all harmful things. Ha, how wrong I was about that. So I'm saying this, find somebody to love for the right reasons. Looking back, I fell in love with the uniform, not the man. It's as if I've been living in a corridor, Robyn, a narrow, dark place.'

Claudia looked tired, I suggested she get some rest, and we could catch up the next day; she seemed relieved, said she could do with a lie down.

When I got in, Alex wasn't around. Derek opened the front door to me, used his whole body to block the hall, arm stretched across to the bannister. I had no choice but to run straight upstairs. At the Pier Head, for a moment, I was tempted to ask Claudia about staying with her in the Adelphi. But it sounded cheeky and she had her own problems to sort out. I went into the bathroom; took the new toothbrush out of my pocket, got a wash, brushed my teeth slipped inside the covers still wearing my clothes. Sunday tomorrow, I'd need to be up early; I was meeting Claudia.

The front door slammed; the sound of footsteps coming up the stairs. From the streetlight outside I could see on my watch it was twenty to four. The footsteps stopped outside my room. I closed my eyes, turned on my side and faced the wall. The room door opened. I could smell beer. Thought it must be Alex but wouldn't let him know I was awake. I heard the gentle click of the catch, let out a breath, turned back around again. Alex was standing next to my bed watery eyes looking down at me, he was drunk.

He stood there, reaching out a hand towards my face. I turned away, faced the wall for what seemed like an age.

Finally, I heard the twist of the door handle.

My one wish right now, was to be able to take a bubble bath. To run the hot water, take all of my clothes off and step in, have a good soak. Instead I had to wash myself in the little sink, standing in front of the mirror in the bathroom, a cat's lick Nan called it. Wash my underwear through in the bathroom sink; lift the chair over by the window in the bedroom, open it wide and hope the wind would dry them.

Just thinking about a hug from Nan made my chest tremble. I should have asked Stella for one more week, give me time to find something better. Tomorrow, maybe Claudia would let me pay something towards staying in the Adelphi with her, especially if her room had two single beds. I'd give all of my wages, if that's what it would take to make her say yes.

34

Derek opened the front door as I was going out, carrying his newspaper. He blocked the doorway so I couldn't get past.

'What you gonna do once that scheme of yours finishes?' His voice held a coolness in it; a touch of shade.

'Scheme?'

He gave me a sarcastic smile. 'The work scheme, Alex tells me it's up soon.'

'March.'

'That's soon. Nobody lives here who doesn't work, none of that nonsense here. What do you think's gonna happen when you have no money to support yourself?'

'I don't know. I want to work.'

'You have something lined up?'

'Not yet.'

'Then start looking. You think you can sponge off other people in life you're wrong.' He folded his arms across his chest; the rolled-up newspaper stuck out like a sword. 'You'll make enemies faster than a prime minister; you listening to me?'

I nodded; his lips were thick and rubbery-looking as if constantly being stung by the venom inside his words.

'But I want to work.'

'I'm talking about laziness, nasty business to get into. Addictive it is, once you form the habit, it's difficult to kick. You understand?'

'Yes.'

'It's all right saying yes then the next minute you go sponging off social security. I've always worked, always paid my taxes.' Spit dropped onto his shirt like acid. 'I won't have any giros being shoved through this letterbox. Don't want any of that nonsense here. Let's get one thing straight,' he poked me in the chest with the paper, 'there's no way you're using this address.'

'Don't touch me you horrible get.'

'I didn't touch you.'

'You just hit me with that paper.'

'Prove it. You'll get nowhere with lies like that, and swearing at me won't work either.'

'Who swore?'

'You did; mouth like a fucking sewer.'

His tongue was a shovel that dug words up and hurled them into the air like worms. I squeezed past him, made my way down the front path, the bones in my legs felt weak. He was shouting more stuff at me, people walking past stopped to stare. He did hit me, the creep; I thought about telling Alex, realised he probably wouldn't believe me.

At the Adelphi Hotel, the table was square; set for four people. We had real napkins and huge shiny, silver knives and forks. A waiter came to our table and Claudia ordered a glass of red wine. I ordered orange juice, thought of the tall tale I'd fed Dot, and smiled. We read the menu; Claudia said she'd try the roast dinner. Everything cost a fortune.

I thought about Nan, and Grandad, dining here on their twenty-fifth wedding anniversary, wondered what table they sat at? They might have sat right here, in this very place all those years ago, "Best night out of my life," Nan had said.

'Order whatever you want, my treat.'

'You sure?'

'Of course.'

'I'll have the same as you, please.'

The dining room was huge. Crystal chandeliers dangled from the high ceiling. The carpets were thick and bouncy under my shoes. There were crystal glasses on every table and real white tablecloths, not those plastic ones that everything sticks to, not too far away from what I'd told Dot.

'It's a grand hotel, Robyn.'

'Gorgeous, my nan and granddad spent their twenty-fifth anniversary here, and Nan worked here years ago.'

'Did they? That's amazing. How old are you, Robyn?'

'I'll be seventeen next week.'

'You've got your whole life ahead of you. Do you live with your mum now?'

'No, she lives in Edinburgh.'

'I'm sorry to hear that. You must have been close to your nan.'

'I was.'

'You don't like the idea of Edinburgh?'

'I'm better off making my own way.'

'Do you live with your dad?'

'No, I don't know where he is. I live with a friend.'

'But you're okay?'

'Yes,' I lied. I'd speak to her about staying in the hotel after we'd had our dinner. I was excited, hoping she'd say yes.

Claudia flapped her napkin open. 'I'm off to London in the morning, going to see if I can find my sister.'

I tried to keep the disappointment out of my voice. 'Oh, I thought you needed time to think.'

'I got through a lot of thinking last night, about my options. I'm choosing not to be scared of life any more. I want to find my sister.'

Claudia carried on talking but I didn't hear the words, she was my last chance. I thought about packing my bags and living on the streets. The weather was still cold, especially at night, and I'd end up scabby, and stinking, lose my job in Waterford's before I had the reference.

I needed to contact my dad. Then I thought what if he was dead? He might have been killed. Even if he was dead I'd keep making him up. In every stranger's face, I'd keep searching for my own.

The waiter brought our drinks; Claudia looked so happy now she knew what she was going to do.

'Write to me once you get to London?'

She took a little notebook out of her bag. 'Okay, I will, write your address down.'

'I'm moving soon. Why don't you send it to Waterford's? Just write my name on the envelope and Maud, our manageress, will pass it on.'

She smiled. 'I'd like us to stay in touch.'

'Where will you start your search?'

'I know she worked in Harrods in the ladies' underwear department. I have the address I sent her last Christmas card to years ago; it's a wild goose chase, I know. But if I do find Denise, it'll be worth the trouble. I got on with her well when we were younger. There was only the two of us, and we're very close in age, only twelve months between us, but she didn't get along with my husband. And we are family, I often think about her.'

I thought about my dad all of the time.

'What's on your mind, Robyn?'

'Nothing, what time are you leaving?'

'I'm getting the first train out. I'll keep in touch, promise, post you a letter in a week or so, let you know how I'm getting on.'

'I hope you find her, Claudia.'

'So do I, but you know, even if I don't, at least I can tell myself I tried. London's a big place, much bigger than Liverpool.'

'You'll find her.'

Claudia stood up, came over to the side of my chair and hugged me, 'Thank you. You've been a real friend to me. I don't expect everything to be plain sailing. I know my husband, he won't let me have my freedom this easily; he'll come looking. I'll just have to be extra careful.'

When we'd finished eating, Claudia folded the address to Waterford's up, tucked it away in her bag, we said goodbye to each other. Outside, I felt the darkness filling up my head like a giant stone.

I took a walk, as far away from Alex's house as I could get; didn't plan on going back there until late.

The front door to Nan's old place was shut tight, like the front cover of an unread book; and the street, a shelf full with old words and old songs. Outside the block, I sat on the fence for ages; nobody came out of their homes. I was tempted to knock at Betty's, changed my mind.

An old man eventually came out of Nan's place, with his arm

around a woman. They walked past me like I wasn't there, new breath in our old rooms where we once ate, and laughed, and read, and sang. When it got cold I checked my watch, five to eleven. The easiest thing would be to just sit here until whenever, but I had to wash my overall for work in the morning.

On Scotland Road, the number 3 bus was already there. I sat down, from the window saw a few people coming out of a pub, the Throstle's Nest. In amongst the crowd, I spotted him, a pulse raced in my chest. Pulling the little window across I shouted: 'Bernie! Bernie!'

God, I hadn't seen him in years, saying his name out loud made a hot feeling fill up my throat. He looked around, but in the opposite direction, didn't see me. Lovely Bernie; who'd looked out for me when I lived in Tommy Whites. A girl stumbled out of the pub, linked her arm through his.

'You wanna get off the next stop, girl?' The driver shouted.

'No,' I said, sinking down in my seat, 'it doesn't matter.'

How I wanted to get off the frigging bus, run over to Bernie, and give him the biggest hug. It was clear he'd found someone, had probably forgotten all about me.

Derek was doing something to the front door with his tools. He saw me, put on his solemn funeral face.

'You been messing with this latch?'

'No.'

The bulb had gone in the hall, he stooped down, torch in his hand; squinting at the lock while he spoke. 'Well somebody has. You know how much a new front door costs?'

'Eight pounds?'

He got in close to my face. I could smell tobacco and coffee, 'You being funny?'

'No,' I said, my voice a whisper, 'I'm not being funny.'

'I should throw your clothes into the street. This is your last warning; I mean it, you're going to see a different side to me.' He put down his tools and turned away; walked down the path, unzipped his trousers, leaned back and pissed against the fence.

Before he turned around I ran straight upstairs; pushed the top of the chair tight against the handle of the door, sat on the edge of the bed. I couldn't figure him out, but knew he was about to lose it with me, how his eyes grew wild, the mad way he looked. Maybe there was a safe place on the streets that I hadn't found yet, anything would be better than this.

35

Stella was filling in the returns sheet. Loads of stock left over today, we'd been dead quiet. I still managed to give two customers the wrong change. Maud got a nark on and told me to take a longer dinner.

'It's your birthday soon, isn't it?' Stella said when I got back. 'Saturday, I'll have the place to myself. The lads and my dad are going away for the weekend with some football club. I could throw a small party for you, for your seventeenth.'

'I've never had a party.'

'It's settled, then. Invite Rose and the lads and their mates. Not too many. Eight to ten of us should be plenty.'

'Okay, thanks.'

Maud handed me the first letter from Claudia. She was still looking for her sister in London. She didn't find her through work, or her address, she was going through the phone book, ringing all of the women who were named Denise Seabrook. Claudia was renting a flat in the north of London in a place called Camden, was looking for a job and she liked it there. I tucked the letter away in my overall pocket, a fresh start in a brand new place and she was happy. I hoped she'd find her sister.

On Saturday morning, Rose was in Curl Up-n-Dye, busy shampooing a lady when I walked in. Paula told me to sit down and wait. When Rose had finished, she called me into the back. 'Nice mate you are,' she said. 'Haven't seen you for ages, didn't even know you'd moved.'

'Sorry, it was a rush, Stella wanted to leave Norm's and I felt…'

'Where're you living now?'

'Alex has let me stay in his for a couple of weeks, until I find somewhere else.'

'His parents let you?'

'He just lives with his dad, but he's a strange man, sixpence short of a shilling, Nan would've said. I'm looking for somewhere else. I don't eat there; it's just a place to sleep.'

Then I remembered, 'Stella's throwing a party for my seventeenth, Saturday.'

'Ahh, is she, can't wait!' Rose clapped.

On my way to Alex's, I stopped at a phone box. The phone book sat on a black shelf, tied to the wall with thick string. Searching for the letter N, I slid my finger down the list until I came to R, picked up the handset and dialled the number for the first R. Naylor I found. The machine beep beeped for the money. I heard the coin clunk down into the box. A kid answered the phone and said, hello.

'Hello, is your dad there, please?'

'Daaaad, phone.'

A deep voice said, 'Hello?'

I said nothing.

'Hello, who is it?'

I closed my eyes tried to picture his face, brown hair, blue eyes.

'Anyone there?'

'Hello, erm, I might have the wrong number but did you ever know a girl called Robyn?'

'Never heard of any Robyn, sorry.'

I let my finger fall below to the second R. Naylor; dialled the number, this time there was no answer. I ran to the sweet shop across the road and bought myself a pen; ran back to the phone box and drew a little ring around the no answer name. I opened the door and looked outside, checked nobody was looking, tore out all of the pages with Naylor written on, stuffed them inside my coat pocket.

Sitting down on the number 3 bus, I closed my eyes, hadn't been sleeping well in Alex's; and didn't feel safe. My dad, if I could find him, might be able to help me find a place to live. I'd like to meet him; hoped he'd want to see me. What if that first man who came to the phone was my dad? What if he just said he wasn't, to get rid of me? What if I spent all of my money on phone calls trying to track down a person who didn't want to be found? Then I thought of Claudia trying to find her sister, she was right about one thing; even if he wanted nothing to do with me, at least I could say I'd tried.

I got off the bus, took a walk around town; looked in a couple of second-hand shops at the bags and the dresses. The stuff was cheaper than Claudia's shop in Southport, except there was nothing worth buying. I sat in a café near the Adelphi, ordered a pot of tea; took the pages out of my pocket, sat there for ages reading all of the different names and addresses and wondering if any of them were my dad's.

Inside a phone box, I dialled the second R. Naylor's number; still no answer. I tried the third number, an old lady answered; she sounded sweet. I asked her if she knew Robert Naylor. She said no, her husband's name was Raymond Naylor, but he died two years ago. She asked me my name, then she started talking about her husband, and how he was a magician, and he'd won awards for his work, and once, he did a show for George Formby, when it was his wife's fortieth birthday.

She went through a list of names of other famous people I didn't know. She talked so much the beeps went, I had to keep feeding the slot, listening to the life story of a dead man I'd never met. Eleven minutes later she finally hung up to pee, and I was almost skint.

Back at Alex's, Derek opened the door and I gave him my keep. He took the money and walked away. 'Have you got a spare key?' I asked.

'What for?'

'I'm going to a party Saturday, then out with my mate afterwards. I might be back late. Don't want to wake anybody up.'

He went into the kitchen, came back with a spare key. 'I didn't get a key until I was twenty-one,' he said. 'Don't come rolling back here rotten drunk all hours in the morning.'

'I won't. I only have enough money for two drinks.'

He looked in his palm, 'You moaning about paying too much here?'

'No, I mean, I won't be drunk, I won't be able to…'

'If that's what you think you can take your money and sling your hook, that's the trouble with ungrateful bitches.'

'I'm not paying too much. The keep is all right.'

He stepped towards me. 'All right, what do you mean by all right?'

I backed away from him, everything I said he twisted around so that it sounded like an accusation, he was getting nastier by the day. Upstairs, in the room, I rammed the chair up against the door, made the bed, scanned the names in the phone book, 'Which one are you?' I said out loud. 'Please, next time, let my eyes fall on the right one.'

36

There was a glass cabinet in the corner of the livingroom filled with football trophies. Stella had set up a table in the kitchen, with ale on one side, and food on the other. She poured me and Rose vodka and coke, buckets more vodka than coke. Stella's eyes were already all wobbly. She told us she had a couple of drinks while she was getting things ready, 'Gets you in the mood.'

'In the mood for what?' I asked, but she didn't answer. She'd put red and yellow balloons up all over the house.

'It looks amazing, Stella. Thanks.'

'Not every day you get to be seventeen. When're the lads coming?'

'About ten Alex said. He's bringing his cousin and his mates, should be about six of them.'

Stella lifted her glass up above her head, 'Cheers, everyone,' she said, 'to a great night.'

Three women Stella went to school with knocked at the door. She poured them a drink, introduced them to me and Rose then took them into the livingroom. We could hear them screaming laughing through the wall. When the music stopped, Rose put a Blondie album on.

'She's got a Bryan Ferry one here. I'll put him on next.'

We danced around the kitchen with our drinks. Stella came in to fill up glasses, she joined in with us. Then the other three girls came to find Stella, soon all six of us were dancing, singing along with the records and laughing.

It had gone eleven o'clock when Alex turned up with a gang of lads. I could tell by Alex's eyes, he was already drunk. I left them in the kitchen, went into the livingroom and talk to Jenny, one of Stella's mates from school. She told me they were staying another half an hour, but she wanted to try and get one of the girls to go to Gatsby's with her. There was a lad she fancied, and she knew he'd be out tonight.

After a bit Alex sat next to me on the settee. 'Happy birthday,' he put his arm around me, leaned in for a kiss. I turned so he got my cheek. Jenny left the room to get herself something to eat.

'Always playing hard to get, aren't you?' Alex said. 'Think you're too good for anyone.'

I stood up, tried to change the subject. 'Where've you been, town?'

'I'm not good enough for the likes of you?'

'That's rubbish and you know it. I thought we'd said-'

He stood up. 'What? Friends and all that shit? Ha! That's what you said, not me. Dick-teaser,' he walked away.

I went into the kitchen and poured myself a drink, couldn't believe what he'd just called me. Rose was talking to Harry over by the record player. A couple of the girls were dancing with lads I didn't know. Back in the livingroom I had a dance with Jenny to Bryan Ferry, *Love is the Drug*.

The downstairs bathroom was full. Upstairs, I heard giggles

coming from inside a bedroom. The door was open a little and I could see inside. Stella was sitting on the edge of the bed, leaning back. She still had her skirt on but her blouse and her bra were on the floor. Her head was flung right back. Alex knelt down, kissing one of her breasts. I ran downstairs into the kitchen, Rose was kissing Harry.

Tears filled up my eyes. I blinked them away, went back into the livingroom and sat with Jenny, couldn't get the picture of Stella and Alex to go away. Stella was my friend. I didn't understand how she could do that. Especially after all the stuff she'd said about her mum.

With only two weeks of my scheme left at Waterford's, even if they offered me a permanent job now, with double pay, I wouldn't take it; didn't want to be in the same room as Stella or Alex if I could help it.

37

Sunday, it had gone three o'clock in the afternoon. No smell of a roast dinner cooking, no music playing, no table set for dinner, only the muffled sound of the television downstairs. Norm was so special to be around. When I lived with him, out of all of the days in the week, I always looked forward to Sunday. Norm, fussing around the oven door that wouldn't shut properly but still kept the heat in. I had always felt cold in this room with its uncurtained window. One thought kept coming back to me over and over again: I hoped my dad was something like Norm.

I got washed, dressed, brushed my teeth and made the bed; walked downstairs, straight out of the front door. Derek shouted out of the front bedroom window. 'Where's Alex? He didn't come home last night.'

I ignored him.

'Eh, I'm talking to you!' he shouted.

I turned around and shouted back at him, 'Last time I saw your Alex, he was kneeling down sucking on Stella's tit, if you must know!'

See what he had to say about his precious Alex, now.

In the phone box I took out the list. Half an hour later, still no luck. I was about to try another number, when a lady started tapping a coin on the glass.

I opened the door. 'How long will you be? I've been watching out my window, waiting for you to finish, you messing about in there?'

'Yes,' I wanted to say, suddenly feeling lighter. 'I'm ringing Gregory Peck to see if he wants to come to dinner. Then, just for a bloody laugh, I'll try Frankenstein and Elton John.'

I smiled at her angry face, kill them with kindness. 'I'll be two minutes,' I said, 'sorry.' I tried the next number on the list.

A man's voice said, 'Hello?'

'Hello, I might have the wrong number but years ago, did you know a girl called Robyn?'

Silence.

'Hello?' I said.

The lady tapped her coin on the glass again and it made a clickety-clack sound.

I put two fingers up the wrong way, meaning two minutes.

On purpose, she sent two rude fingers back at me.

'I did, yes, many years ago,' he said.

'Sorry? What?' *Oh. My. God.*

'I said I did know a Robyn, many years ago.'

He had a soft voice, this could be him, I thought. Nobody spoke, just the sound of us both breathing.

'Hello, are you still there?'

I gripped the little shelf where the phone book sat. 'Yes, I'm here. Do you know who I am?'

'I think I do.'

'Am I going to get you into any trouble, I'll hang up if I am?'
'Give me a number and I'll ring you back.'
'I don't have a number.'

The lady opened the door. 'You're doing this on purpose. If you don't hurry up, I'm going to phone my son. My son's a policeman.' She slammed the door shut then opened it again fast. 'You've got one minute, don't you dare put another coin in that machine.'

Her son's a policeman? What was that supposed to mean? He'd come along here with handcuffs and arrest me for talking too much on the phone?

'Hello, Robyn, it is you, isn't it?'
'Yes, it's me.'

Beep beep beep. I pushed another coin in the slot.

The door swung open. She snatched the handset and hung up. Squashed herself beside me inside the phone box, kept the tip of her boot on the door so it stayed open. Her breath reeked of fish, salt fish.

'Now, I have an important call to make, madam, if you don't mind, out!' With her foot she opened the door wider. She wore a green pinny and brown boots that zipped up the front. 'Everything in life's not to do with messing about, you know.'

I stepped out of the phone box, waited outside; stood there watching the lady's lips move. She nodded her head, yes, yes. Yes, I knew a Robyn. He didn't say no. He knew my name right away. He said it. He said Robyn. I think he said it.

How many phone boxes had I walked past over the years? All the time my dad's name was in there, right there in the book, and I didn't think until Claudia told me how she was searching for her sister. I took my coin and clickety-clacked it on the glass. The woman threw me a filthy look. 'I've got an important phone call to make,' I said, 'very important.'

On the shelf inside the phone box I could see my torn out list. Finally, the woman hung up. I opened the door wide.

She held out the list, wafted it in my face. 'Did you tear pages out of this book?'

No answer.

'Did you?'

'Yes.'

'That's a punishable offence, defacing public property. That book's not yours to tear. How would you like it if I came to your house and started tearing pages out of your book? You wouldn't like it would you?'

'Somebody already tore pages out of my book. I'm trying to get them back.'

I snatched the paper from her hand.

'Bleedin' twerp,' she said. 'Anyone would think it was your phone box.'

I looked at the BT sign. 'It is my phone box, look here's my initials: bleedin' twerp.' I went inside, slammed the door shut; dialled the number.

He picked up straight away. 'What happened?'

His voice: a small and irreplaceable thing inside the black receiver.

'Some woman needed the phone.'

'Where are you?'

'Near Liverpool town centre.'

'I'll meet you tomorrow.'

'Where?'

'Wherever's best for you.'

'Outside the Adelphi?'

'All right.'
'Seven o'clock?'
'I'll be there. I'll wear my suit, my grey suit.'
'Brown hair and blue eyes?'
'Blue eyes, yes, what hair I've got left is going grey now.'
I smiled, heard the beeps again. 'Okay, bye.'
'Bye, Robyn.'

38

She stayed close to Maud all morning, but when Maud left for her dinner, it'd just be me and her. Then I wanted to hear what she had to say, to find out if there was anything left of our friendship.

Maud sensed something was wrong. 'You two are unusually quiet? I need to get some air, taking an early dinner.'

A couple of customers came in and we served them. After they'd gone I turned to Stella and looked at her straight. She made an excuse to go to the toilet. After what seemed like ages she came back.

'Robyn, I don't know what to say.'

'About you being a slag you mean?'

'Now look, I know I shouldn't have gone with him, don't even fancy him or anything. I was drunk. It's not like you're with him anyway, and the ale, I wasn't thinking straight.'

'You're such a hypocrite.'

'You don't want him, so that means nobody else can have him, is that what you're saying?'

'I thought you were my friend, you're nothing but a…'

'Open that trap of yours again, holy fuckin' Mary, and you'll end up being launched through that window.'

'Try it, go on, think I'll just stand here and let you?'

She lunged at me. I blocked her arm, reached forward into the glass counter, picked up a family-sized trifle, turned and smashed it, *splat*, into Stella's face. It felt good. Cream lodged inside her lashes, on her eyelids, yellow custard dripped from her fringe in goopy blobs.

Maud walked in, she'd forgotten her purse. Saw Stella covered in trifle and gasped. Stella took a tissue from the box; wiped her face. Maud told me to stay on the counter, called Stella into the back of the shop. After a few minutes, Maud told me to go on my dinner first.

When I got back Maud said Mr Fairbrother had rang the shop. 'He said he's sorry, Robyn, but they won't be keeping you on after all. They can't afford to at the moment.'

Stella put her coat on, smirked at me then left for her dinner.

'That's all right Maud,' I said. 'It's not your fault. I didn't want to stay on here, anyway.'

'I'm sure you'll find something. I'll get cracking on your reference; make sure it's all-singing and all-dancing.'

'Will it be all right if I call in now and again after I've left, in case my friend, Claudia, writes me a letter?'

'Of course it is. I'll keep them for you. Why don't you write to her with your own address?'

'I'm moving soon. But once I'm settled, I won't have to use this address.'

I looked out of the window. Across the road, saw Alex and Stella walking towards town. She was linking him. I looked away before they saw me. Maud was at my side.

'I'll pay for the trifle,' I said, 'but I'm not sorry.'

'No need. They aren't going to last,' she said. 'I can tell.'

'How?'

'There's a half-baked look about them. Two thin crackers dipping themselves into hot water. Fall to mush, they will, once the temperature changes. It's pretty cheap what they're doing. Robyn, you're a treasure, and he doesn't deserve you.'

It surprised me to know Maud felt like that, she'd never said much, not to me anyway.

'Thank you,' I said.

Stella was probably right, why should I care if Alex was going with someone else. Didn't I tell him we were friends now, and all that? Part of me was still hoping I'd see something in him that'd convince me he'd never scare me again. Foolish to think he might wait until I was ready. That wasn't the way life worked.

It had been one of those sunny, end of February days, the false promise of warmer weather had gone; blustery winds tore new petals loose from the branches. They gathered in packs on the steps of the Adelphi, like old confetti; still a gorgeous shade of pink that deserved its place in full light.

Climbing up the Adelphi steps, goosebumps formed on my skin. I wished I'd put a coat on over my dress. The man on the door, dressed up in a military uniform, shouted over to me. 'It's not spring yet, you know. There's still the chance of a freeze.'

After about half an hour of standing in the cold, I thought he's not coming, walked over to the man on the door of the Adelphi; asked him if I could use the toilet. He said yes, told me to come straight back out. I put the lid down on the toilet seat; sat there for a bit, trying to get warm, washed my hands with soap and warm water, looked in the mirror, straightened my dress. Then

I thought why bother? Why bother with any of this? He's not coming. I looked into my flared-up face and said, *you silly, stupid cow; who the hell were you kidding?*

Outside, the man said, 'You still waiting for someone?'

'I was, but I'm not now.'

'Maybe a few more minutes before you give up? You never know, the lad might've been in an accident, or be helping somebody else whose had an accident.'

I laughed and cried at the same time, but it came out more of a laugh, 'Yeah, best to look on the bright side, eh?'

He smiled, 'Nah, you know what I mean. What's your name?'

'Robyn.'

'Mine's Kenneth, Ken to you.'

Then he started telling me about the hotel, and about how, at one time, they had fifty-six bell boys and porters. 'They'd pick up people's bags from Lime Street Station and carry them back here to the hotel. We had ballroom dancers. The men always wore tails or dinner jackets. And the ladies, now then, those dresses were grand.'

'I'd like to have seen them.'

'It was a grand sight all right. Things aren't the same now.'

I wondered what people would do if they ever ran out of stories to tell?

I checked my watch.

'What time was the meeting?'

'Seven.' He was nearly one hour late.

Ken said nothing, just smiled and shook his head.

'Think I'll go. Nice meeting you.'

'You too, young lady, good luck.'

I walked away fast before he saw me crying. Disappointment was a funny thing. If I thought things were always going to turn out like this, I'd honestly give up trying. It didn't feel as bad once you expected it. This time I didn't, and I thought of the word *empty*. Empty was a shelf underneath a heart, it expected nothing but when it got something good, it sang. Like when I met Rose and Norm and Claudia. I was stronger for meeting people like them, much, much stronger. And Nan, who may have taken all the untold stories with her; but while she was here, the tender way she was with me, made me feel like I mattered, a feeling that stirred inside me whenever I thought of her. I tried hard to keep that feeling alive.

The rest of the week in work was all about trying not to speak to Stella. She did exactly the same to me. Maud got a nark on and told us both to sort things out. When Saturday came, I ran down to Curl Up-n-Dye to see Rose. She called me into the back.

'How's it going with Harry?'

'He's all right, you know. I could do worse, what about Alex?'

I told her about him and Stella.

'That's nasty,' she said. 'You'd never think that of Stella, would you? Mind you, I can talk; look what the ale did to me, ending up preggy.'

'I know, love. Next week's my last in Waterford's. I need my reference off Maud.'

'Wanna to go out tonight? We could share something to eat, go and see a film.'

'All right, meet you outside the Adelphi at half eight?'

'Okay.'

On my way into town I walked past the phone box where I'd spoken to my dad. There was nobody inside. I opened the door; took the list out of my pocket. He really did sound like he wanted to meet me. Maybe that man at the Adelphi was right, maybe something had happened. I dialled the number, to give it one last try, pushed the coin into the slot.

A man's voice answered, 'Hello?'

I said nothing.

'Is that you, Robyn?'

'What happened?'

'Sorry. I've had a bug.'

'Sorry to hear that.'

'Thursday, what about this Thursday, lunch time?'

Thursday was the day before I finished in Waterford's. 'All right, Thursday, outside the Adelphi?'

'Twelve o'clock, outside the Adelphi, midday. I won't let you down, promise.'

Did every false promise leave a scar?

This could be some crazy story he'd thought up to get me off the phone. He was probably getting his phone number changed any day now. It was no big deal to me, Thursday at twelve. I wouldn't go over to the Adelphi until I saw him through Waterford's window.

'Okay, see you then.'

That night, I went for a meal with Rose, to the Golden Dragon restaurant in town. We shared a curry with rice and a portion of chips. We talked about our years together in school, had a laugh remembering the teachers, and about some of the girls Rose had battered. When they came with the hot flannels, Rose looked at me and smiled, then we started laughing, forgot all about the film and, at midnight, Rose said she was going to meet Harry outside Cindy's.

Before we left, I told her about my dad and how I was supposed to be meeting him on Thursday. She didn't believe me at first, but when I finally convinced her, she said, 'I hope he turns up for you, Robyn. You deserve to find him, and who knows what might happen?'

I knew she meant that I might find a real home. But she didn't say it and neither did I. It was too much to hope for, too much like an impossible thing to find.

I was in bed wearing cords and a sweatshirt when the room door opened. It was still dark outside, at first I thought it was Derek and I screamed. Then I saw Alex, swaying.

He lifted the little chair, sat down by the window. Leaned back on the damp underwear I'd washed through in the sink.

'Why are you here?' he said.

I didn't know what to do, so I said nothing. If he came near me, I'd kick him in the nuts and scream the frigging house down.

'This some kind of sick game you're playing?'

I sat up. 'Why don't you beat it back to Stella?'

He leaned over, jiggled the window open as wide as it would go; stood up, grabbed a handful of second-hand dresses from the wardrobe. 'You think more of these dead things.' Without taking them off the hangers, he ripped each dress down from the neckline, one at a time, flung them out of the window.

He carried on, until there were no dresses left, looked at me, tossed the chair over by the window, opened the room door, and left.

I heard his room door slam, picked my underwear up off the floor; looked out of the window. The dresses were scattered all over the yard. Some of them had twisted and wrapped around one another, lying there, like dead bodies.

Every time I wore each dress, I would make up a story about

the woman who first bought it; where she went, who she was with. I had been wearing other people's clothes, stepping inside other people's lives, because my own life was too painful. I saw that now. Alex flinging the dresses away made me more determined to learn how to sew, make my own clothes. New clothes, made to fit my body, not somebody else's; clothes that would never have to be altered or hidden away at the back of a shop, shoved onto the damaged rail.

The way he'd looked at me, I was a disappointment, not what he'd expected; a mistake. Or was that how I looked at him? The truth was I didn't want to get close to Alex or anybody. I lived in a world full of uncertainty, and walking away without owing anybody anything would be half the battle. There was plenty of time for being responsible for somebody else. For now, it was easier if I was on my own, because nothing else lasted.

39

Maud tipped the float into the till, nudged the draw shut with her hip; leaned forward across the counter, hands clasped, waiting for the first customer. I watched the morning sun crawl across the cakes in the window. A customer opened the shop door, a slight breeze pushed the smell of icing towards me.

The return of mornings filled with sunlight made my thinking become scattered. I remembered Nan, and summers spent in her back garden, under the communal washing line, talking and listening to her stories.

On days like these I almost forgot that Nan had died. Then the memory of her came back, attached to it a string of questions, and things I never told her. I imagined her living, just for five more minutes, felt the way I used to feel. Five minutes was all I'd need, to tell her how good and funny, and important she was, and how I often talked to myself, asked questions of advice, and it was Nan's voice and words that came with the answers. In that moment I persuaded myself that she was still close by, in those small moments, still here with me.

Alex and Stella met every day now on their dinner. Stella

saw me looking at them together yesterday, it was like she wasn't bothered if I saw them or not. She grinned back at me and I felt like slapping her face.

The month of March was true to its name: a month that did not dawdle or mope around like January; but marched away from itself towards the sweetness of summer. Time was running out for me, if my dad wasn't at the Adelphi this week, I didn't know what I was going to do, probably end up sleeping on a bench again. What was I thinking? No. I was never going back to that.

Another letter came from Claudia. She'd got an interview for a job doing alterations in a small dress shop. She was asking for my new address. I wouldn't write back to her until I had one, didn't want to have to come back to Waterford's ever again.

Maud had grown different. She didn't look me in the eye when she spoke. Told me to take longer than an hour on my dinner, and not to bother writing down what I ate this week. I knew she felt sorry for me, and it was her way of making it up to me, and to feel better about how things had turned out.

I wrote everything down and came back from my dinner after one hour. Not because I wanted to be nasty to her, I hated people feeling sorry for me. I'd had that most of my life. Nan was happy for me, when she found out I'd got this job. She told everyone in the club, she was so proud of me. How unfair it is that Nans are old when kids begin to really know them, and how, in the blink of an eye they disappear, and everything changes forever.

40

Thursday, ten to twelve, the morning had dragged, hardly anybody was in town; the streets were empty. I had a bad feeling in my bones, knew he wouldn't turn up today, either. Why would he? I was a teenager. He'd probably been thinking a new worry to deal with. I hadn't even bothered to ask Maud for the twelve o'clock dinner.

Then, from Waterford's window, I watched a man in a grey suit climb up onto the first step of the Adelphi Hotel. He had glasses on and his hair had some grey, but it was still mostly dark like mine. I couldn't stop staring, unable to move. A few minutes later, Maud said she was going on her dinner, I panicked. 'Can I have the twelve o'clock, Maud, I'm meeting somebody?'

Maud smiled. 'Course you can. Take as long as you like,' she said, 'me and Stella can manage.'

I went to the toilet, put on a bit of lippy, pinched my cheeks, grabbed my coat and ran across the road. I walked past Ken, he shouted hello after me. Smiling at him, I waved. Walking up onto the first few steps, I said to the man with the bits of grey hair, wearing glasses, 'Is your name, Robert?'

His eyes widened once he saw me, like suddenly finding a

hidden bruise, hands deep inside pockets, shoulders up to his ears, 'Robyn?'

I nodded. We both stood there unsure what to do next. He took a big breath, puffed out his cheeks, then stepped away, as if to see me better. 'You're the spit of our Pat,' he said, in his soft voice.

'Pat?'

'Your aunty, shall we get a cup of tea somewhere?'

We found a little café inside Lewis's; I got the table while he got the tea. I looked carefully at his face. His skin was not thick, but pale and papery, like mine. And it was in this simple detail, that, for the first time in my life, I recognised myself in somebody else. He sat opposite me, pulled his chair up tight to the table. I could only smell aftershave on him. No smoke. For some reason I thought he'd smoke.

'How long's your break?'

'I have an hour,' I said.

One hour. To dig up the past, offer it a seat next to us; toss it up in the air like a win or lose coin. *Heads*, it gets ugly and we never see each other again. *Tails*, we... but that was me, jumping the gun again.

'Let's just wait and see,' Nan would say. *'Wait and see.'*

'Are you all right?' he said.

'I'm fine.'

'I'm not sure what you've been told, but I wanted to meet you, to let you know I came back for you.'

He picked up the pot and poured my tea first.

I watched the steam rise up towards his face. 'Did you?'

'No, yes, I mean...' He slammed the pot down a bit too hard. 'Sorry, I'm not proud of what happened, your mother didn't tell you?'

'She never spoke about you, never let me speak about you.' I didn't tell him Nan had done some digging and found out he had two children.

'Things happened, in the past, you know, I wasn't ready…'

I said nothing, poured milk into my cup.

'My thinking was, once you were old enough, you could make your own mind up.'

Jumbled, mad questions rose in my head like pastry, questions like: Have you got more than two kids now?

'Are you working?'

'Yes.' I could hear in my own voice the wateriness of the words, thin and runny like lies. 'I have a job, over there, in Waterford's bakery, but that finishes tomorrow it was a six month government scheme.'

'They're not keeping you on?'

'No. Does Pat know about me?'

'Yes.'

'Oh.'

'Pat wants to meet you. She lives near town.'

'She does?'

'I told her, after you rang the first time. She said if you ring back, she'd like to meet you. Pat's older than me; she's fifty now, an easy one to be with. You'll like her. She works up London Road, in Selway's Bingo. She's the manageress.'

I thought about that night, and kissing Alex when he walked me for a taxi, before I really knew him. 'I know where that is.'

'Go in any time.'

When he asked the next question, he kept his eyes low down so I couldn't see them. 'How's your mum?'

'Okay. She lives in Edinburgh with this man, Owen.'

'Oh, she's not with…

'No.'

'And how's May?'

I pushed my cup away, no longer wanting the tea. All of the stolen hours and minutes aching, now, deep inside my bones, with the weight of seventeen years. 'Erm, so, yeah, she died.'

Silence.

'Ahh, no, sorry to hear that, she was lovely, May. That's a shame. I'd hoped to meet her again.'

To get to this moment, I had pulled myself through so much, to meet this man, this stranger sitting opposite me who was my father. It would be so easy to blame him for everything. What was the most important thing I wanted him to know?

'I don't think badly of you,' I said.

His eyes were shiny with water. 'You don't?'

'No.'

'You must have been angry with me?'

There were nights when I'd wondered how somebody could walk away from their own child, and not even try to come back to check that they were all right. But these were not thoughts I could tell anybody about. These were thoughts I had stacked up neatly on top of one another and then squashed.

'You lived with May?'

'Yeah, I was always with her.'

'She was nice to me; despite…I'm so sorry, Robyn. A shock for you, eh?'

'She gave me your name, years ago, just in case.'

'Who do you live with now?'

'A friend's letting me stay until I find somewhere else.'

'I can help, speak to Pat for you?'

I couldn't answer that, it was too much to hope for.

'There was only one reason I left my number in the phone

book, you know, in case one day, you might want to get in touch with me.'

Before I left Waterford's, I told myself not to cry, because I'd look weak and needy and he'd hate that. I made an excuse and went to the toilet, blinked the tears away before he saw, didn't want him to think I wasn't strong, or think I couldn't look after myself.

When I got back, he'd written his phone number down, even though I already had it, told me to ring him whenever I wanted. When he looked up, something was missing, like he was listening to a far off conversation I couldn't hear.

'Do you know how it feels to realise you've been cheated out of something important? It must have been spring, the last time I saw you. It's the greatest feeling to finally meet you again.'

Back at work, I served people on the counter, wrote out the returns, brushed the floor; cleaned the glass counter with soapy water and tissue paper, at five o'clock, put on my coat.

I walked up to London Road, stood outside Selway's Bingo for over an hour, eventually, I pushed open the door. The hallway had thick dark red carpet and cream walls. I took the escalator up to the first floor. There was row upon row of tables and chairs; hundreds of them; slot machines flashed on one side of the room.

Behind me a lady was making sandwiches at a snack bar. Up ahead, women queued for their tickets. At the very back of the hall, there was a bar raised up on its own platform, and at the front, a high stage with an oblong box in the middle, filled with white plastic balls, black numbers printed on them. In the bar, a couple of women sat alone having a drink and reading the paper.

Here they were, all the women who couldn't go into a bar on their own, wouldn't go and watch a film in the cinema alone. They had so many choices here, and all under the one roof.

Behind the bar I saw a lady with dark hair like mine.

'Is your name Pat?' I said.

'No, love, go back down to the main desk, she's probably in her office. Ask somebody on the counter selling the books; they'll get her for you.'

I walked back down the steps. Groups of women, young and old, had set out cigarettes, matches, pens on their tables. Some queued at the little kiosk that sold tea, coffee and sandwiches. Some dropped coins into a slot machine. I could only see one man in the whole place. A lady selling books knocked on the wooden door behind her. 'Pat,' she said, 'someone to see you.'

Pat was tall with dark hair; she had a wide smile, and wore glossy cherry brandy lippy. 'Can I help you?' she said.

'My name's Robyn. You wanted to see me?'

She smiled, lifted the end bit of the counter up; tilted her head for me to walk through to the other side.

Once we were in her office she closed the door and threw her arms around me, 'It's great to finally meet you again,' she said. 'It must've been hard for you to contact your dad, taking that step into the unknown.'

No words again, just stupid tears.

'I'm your aunty Pat,' she could see me crying. 'I'm not that ugly am I?'

I laughed. And Pat laughed with me.

She told me to take a seat. 'Tell me what's been happening with you, I want to know everything; your mum wouldn't let me see you. I did try. Last time I held you, you were three days old.'

I didn't know that. I looked at her big cherry brandy smile and thought there's no way I could tell her everything. It would be too much. I told her about living with Nan, and about Mum in Edinburgh, and about Norm, and a little bit about where I was living now. Then I told her Derek didn't want any giros coming through his door. So, after tomorrow, there would be no job and no place to live.

The phone on her desk rang. She didn't pick it up. It rang and rang and rang. She took hold of my hands. When the phone stopped ringing she said, 'Is that so? We'll see about that. I'll be speaking to your dad tonight about you coming to live in mine, has he mentioned it already, would that be okay with you?'

I just sat there, unable to say anything.

41

My last day at Waterford's; Maud had bought me a black handbag as a goodbye present. I had my clothes and my sewing machine in carrier bags at the back of the shop, and the John Lennon LP. Derek had gone for his morning paper when the taxi pulled up early, he didn't even know I was leaving. The taxi driver was friendly, helped me carry things out of the narrow, coffin-like hallway. I opened the window wide; we sped away, my mind struggling to keep up, as the feeling of being pulled backwards left me.

Pat had a spare bedroom, she said I could stay with her as long as I liked. She had a job ready for me in Selway's bingo. I'd be checking the winning cards to begin with. She said it wasn't a government scheme; but a proper job I could keep as long as I worked hard.

It was nearly four o'clock. Maud said I could go early. She gave me my wages, gave me my reference and gave me a hug. 'Thanks for everything,' she said. 'And good luck, I for one will miss you, Robyn.'

I walked down the narrow passageway where Dot used to

meet Mr Fairbrother. Got my bags out of the little cupboard where we hung our coats. Stella came out of the toilet.

'You going?'

'Yeah, see yer.'

'See yer. And I am sorry.'

She was standing beside Maud at the counter. 'Good luck with your retirement, Maud,' I said.

'Retirement, me? There's life in the old girl yet, five more years at least.' She dropped her arm across Stella's shoulders. 'This one wouldn't know what to do without me. I couldn't burden a young girl with a managerial position, it wouldn't be fair.'

Stella scrunched her eyes up at me, like she'd had strong soap rubbed in them.

'Bye,' I said. 'Thanks for everything.'

Pat was waiting outside. 'C'mon, I've got a couple of hours off, we'll get a taxi and I'll show you your new home.'

We sat on the settee next to each other. Pat had a lovely home. All bright colours and squishy chairs, it reminded me a lot of Norm's. In the corner she had a record player.

My room was cosy and clean; about a ten minute walk from town. 'Use the place like it's your own,' Pat said. 'Did you find that little cupboard behind the door in your room? It's handy for shoes. C'mon I'll show you.'

When we got to the room, Pat looked down at the carrier bags. 'Why haven't you unpacked?'

'I will, but not yet.'

'Why?'

I thought whatever you wanted most in the world, the opposite happened. More than anything else in the world I wanted a home. To want something that bad meant it wouldn't happen, and I'd end up homeless or something. It was okay to want things in life, you just couldn't want them too much or they'd disappear.

'I want to make sure,' I said.

'Make sure?'

'You might change your mind.'

She lifted the carrier bags and tipped them out onto the bed. 'I won't change my mind.'

'I can pay keep.'

'How much can you give before you really give at all?'

'Sorry?'

'Give to yourself first.'

'I-'

'If you could give one thing to yourself, what would it be?'

I realised I had never stepped through a front door and thought I am home. Even in Nan's, she worried somebody would tell the council on me, as I wasn't supposed to be there.

'A home,' I said.

'Okay then. Let yourself think of this place as your home.'

'I'd like to pay my way.'

'We can talk about keep another time. Robyn, what's the matter?'

I stayed quiet for a long time. In the stillness everything slowed down. I sat on the edge of the bed. 'I don't know. I don't know what's wrong. Things don't usually happen as easy as this for me, good things, I mean. And if they do, they never last…'

'I'm not gonna kick you out.'

'What if I mess up?'

'You will mess up, that's okay. We're family, family look out for each other. This is the right place to mess up. I'll be disappointed if you don't find ways to mess up!'

I laughed, then.

'You have to stop worrying and start living. You have to start believing you deserve better.'

'I know.'

She changed the subject. 'Is there anything else you'd like?'

'Can I have a bath?'

'Of course you can. I'll run you one myself.'

She walked towards the door. 'Now put those clothes away in the wardrobe, and I'll see you in a minute.'

I wondered what Mum would make of me finding my dad, and living with his sister?

After my bath, Pat had our tea ready, egg and chips. Then we walked up to Selway's Bingo. Pat asked me to watch what the other workers did for tonight, tomorrow, I was going to start work for real. By about ten o'clock I had a good idea what to do. The only thing was, the place got smoky and made my eyes sting.

'You'll get used to it,' Pat said. 'I'll get you drops.'

'Do you know a place where I could learn to sew?'

'Yes, there's a college up by the Irish Centre. We can go there first thing Monday if that's what you'd like?'

'I would.'

'Okay.'

'I could just work nights in the bingo. I really want to learn how to make things. A friend bought me a machine.'

When I got back to Pat's, I opened up the last letter Claudia had sent me, sat down on the bed and wrote her a letter with my new address. It felt great.

Pat came into the room. 'Your dad's on the phone. He wants to speak to you.' I walked into the livingroom and picked up the handset.

'How've you settled?'

'Fine, she's nice.'

'Told you, if you need -'

'I'm fine.'

'Okay. See you Thursday then?'

'Yeah, Thursday, thanks.'

The following night, when it was time for me to go to work, I walked up towards Selway's bingo, past the Walker Art Gallery, with its tower of steps and silences, across the road, towards the Legs of Man pub.

Under the street lights, I didn't think about Mum, or Rose, or even Dad. I thought about sitting on Pat's step on summer evenings; the concrete warm against my legs, listening to the jumpy tune of an ice cream van, and learning all the words off the John Lennon LP, thinking about changes that would come, which were probably not the changes I imagined living.

The end

ACKNOWLEDGEMENTS

I would like to thank Alan Mahar, of Tindal Street Press, who edited an earlier draft of this novel. Special thanks to Alicia Stubbersfield, who continues to support me with my writing. Thanks to a most generous soul, Rob Bremner, for his incredible photograph on the cover of Imagine Living.

Love and thanks to my husband, John, for his unwavering support.

To Antonia, John, Patrick and Joel, all of my true blessings in life. Thanks are owed to Mary and Bob. I owe warm thanks to Dora and Tommy, and Mary and Peter. Love also to Libby Mackay and Ginni Rawsthorne. To Glendon, for his support and patience. Thanks to Mike Morris, Madeline, and the team at Writing on the Wall, where I got my first break. Christine, Emma, Becky and Amanda Taylor are absolute champions of my work, as are Sarah Hughes, Sandy Farmer, Vicky Anderson, Helen Roberts, Jonathan Taylor, Ian Duhig, Jeff Young, Sally Shaw, Marilyn Mornington, Diana Mather, my amazing students, especially, Rita, Joan, San, Doreen, Aileen, Dawn, Vickie, Katie, Helen, Eryl, Kris, Rekha and Linda. Special thanks to the support given by my readers.

ABOUT THE AUTHOR

Photo by Eireann Sharkey

Deborah Morgan grew up in Liverpool. Her first novel, Disappearing Home, was critically acclaimed, and a #1 Bestseller. Her stories, poetry and stage plays that followed have been shortlisted for prizes. She left primary school teaching to write, and lives with her family in Liverpool, where she is writing a book of humerous poems for children, she also teaches Creative Writing.